THE GHOST STATION

A HARVEY BENNETT STORY

NICK THACKER

CHAPTER 1

HARVEY "BEN" Bennett wanted nothing more than a hot shower and a stack of pancakes. Instead, he got a phone call.

It came in at half past four in the morning. The dull ring rattled across the side table in his motel room, where the only other sounds were the low buzz of a flickering neon sign outside and his own faint snoring.

He'd been staying in Anchorage with his friend, Reggie, but his girlfriend Sarah was in town, and he wanted to give them a bit more space. Julie was back home with their daughter, Hope, and Ben had been enjoying a rare two-week stretch of pure nothingness. It hearkened back to his bachelor days, and while he missed his family, he'd been enjoying the freedom of wandering the streets of Anchorage, visiting every brewery and distillery he could find, and generally lazing around.

He blinked awake with a grunt, snatched the phone, and stared at the caller ID. Unknown number. *Of course.* "Yeah?" he said, voice still thick with sleep.

"Bennett," came a clipped voice on the other end. A man. Formal. Crisp. Probably ex-military from the way he said the name, or — *yep.* It was AI.

Strange, he thought.

Ben pressed the phone tighter to his ear. "Speaking."

"Package inbound," the voice said. *"Check your cell — assistance requested, Greenland research site."*

Definitely an artificial-intelligence voice, but it was *very* good.

Ben's eyelids peeled open wider. "I have no clue what you just said, buddy." He sat up, flicked on the lamp, and looked around for a notepad. "Can we talk in real-people English?"

A breath of annoyance came through the line, a surprisingly human sound. He second-guessed his first assessment. *Maybe this guy's just a robot.* There was a long pause, as if the robot-guy was trying to quickly research how to sound normal. *"Sorry. Name's Chambers. I've got a CSO assignment, immediate. You're the nearest resource with an open schedule."* The voice paused. *"You do have an open schedule, right?"*

Ben let out a snort. "That's not... listen buddy. This isn't how we do things. Who the hell are you, anyway? A spook?"

"I represent someone working for the United States government. Credentials are in the aforementioned package. We just don't have a lot of time, and you came highly recommended."

"Mind telling me what you're trying to get me to walk into?"

The voice ignored him. *"Check your phone for mission docs. Transport leaves in four hours from McChord Field, and I've got a plane waiting in Anchorage to get you there. McChord's in Washington State, in case you were wondering."*

"I'm aware," Ben said. "But what makes you think I'll just pick up and do this? In case you weren't aware, the CSO doesn't *work* for the US government. Or *any* government, for that matter."

"We need your help," the robotic voice said, then hung up.

Ben let the phone drop onto the bed. *Another day, another mystery job.* He rubbed the bridge of his nose, then combed his fingers through his short, dark hair.

"Great," Ben muttered. "Should have joined the circus."

For an ex-park ranger, helping form the Civilian Special Operations seemed like a natural step. He wasn't beholden to anyone except the group, and it was a group made up of his closest friends and his wife. He thought about calling Julie now, just to share the odd interaction.

But first, he wanted to see if this was real. If the robot-guy on the other end of the phone had been telling the truth, he should get —

There it is.

His phone buzzed, a text message containing a link.

He hopped out of bed, grabbed his jacket, and made a quick mental inventory while he opened the link. Coordinates, short briefing notes, a contact named Jillian Shepherd. The Department of Defense was mentioned, but all hush-hush. No sign of the usual bureaucratic rigmarole. That told him the situation was urgent, and that the CSO was, in fact, likely the best operators for the job.

They liked the freedom and automation the civilian group provided, and the powers-that-be who hired them for missions liked the hands-off plausible deniability that came with such an arrangement.

It was usually a win-win situation.

Usually.

Ben eyed the time and groaned. "Four hours. Guess I'll have to skip the pancakes."

He still wasn't sure what this gig was, or if he'd take it, but it might be easy money. He'd call Julie on the way, see if there was any reason not to.

He crammed his gear and clothes into the single duffel it had come out of, tossed on boots, and hightailed it to his truck. Outside, the sky was a bruised purple, a hint of dawn hugging the horizon. He didn't bother checking out of the motel.

The drive to the Anchorage airport's private entrance, and then the flight to McChord Field, was a blur of coffee refills and early-morning phone calls.

There hadn't been much information to go off of in the packet he'd received via text, but a call with Julie had given him hope. She thought the guy was legit, the op was real, and to keep her posted. If it was in fact 'easy money,' and they needed help of some sort, there was no reason not to take the job.

Ben pulled up to a side gate designated for private contractors. A bored guard eyed his credentials, made a quick phone call, then waved him through.

Inside one of the drab, low-slung buildings, a tall woman in a puffy black coat and boots waited for him. She had short, spiky hair, the color of midnight, and a look in her eyes that said she'd be on a plane out of here an hour ago if she could.

"You must be Jillian," he said, crossing the distance in a few brisk steps.

She nodded, didn't bother with a handshake. "Dr. Jillian Shepherd. Part-time consultant for the DoD, full-time scientist at the Greenland research station. Or what's left of it."

Ben cocked his head. "What station? You're the one who's been radioing for help?"

"In a manner of speaking," she said, pulling out a tablet. She flicked through some satellite images. "And I'll answer your other question in time. We had an entire team up there. Four scientists, plus me. Things got... dicey a few days ago. Our secondary outpost went dark. I tried to contact mainline support, but apparently, the DoD got spooked and pulled me out for 'debriefing.' That debriefing was just ferrying me to the states and then asking me questions about what I thought was going on over there. Translation: they want to bury the story."

"And now the story's unburied," Ben said. "I'm curious as to what exactly that story *is*."

She thrust the tablet toward him. Grainy photos showed a small cluster of buildings dwarfed by an endless white expanse. "We're on the western edge of Greenland's ice sheet. Climate research mostly, the boring stuff."

She paused, as if waiting for a response. He just stared at her.

"It's... it was a joke. Sorry. 'Boring,' like boring holes in the ground, to pull out core samples and — sorry, never mind. Anyway, we also take on some side projects. The Department of Defense had a stake in one such project—studying possible pathogens in ancient ice."

Ben shifted.

"And one of the lead scientists found something... unusual."

Ben flipped to the next photo. A test tube chunk of something amber-hued. "Unusual how?"

"We still don't fully know. But we suspect it's a living organism—frozen for at least half a million years. Maybe more. That's not exactly the big deal. The big deal is that it's still viable."

Ben frowned. "Meaning it could infect people?"

She raised both brows. "We think so, yes. If it's what we suspect, it has some nasty traits. Genetic memory, maybe. We have no idea."

He inhaled. "Fantastic. That's all we need, another weird strain of something ravaging through the population." Then he nodded at the next hangar, where a battered cargo plane sat waiting. He let out a sigh, realizing he was already going to commit to the mission. "That's us? I assume the rest of the welcoming committee's inside?"

Jillian set off at a brisk pace. "No, they're waiting for us in Greenland. The pilot's name is Mara, but we're the only passengers. We'll meet up with our local guide, Qannik, who knows the ice there better than anyone. I've got a medic prepped too—Dr. Chuck Davis—because we're not sure what we're dealing with medically."

They walked to the plane, and Ben tossed his duffel into the cargo hold after entering via the lowered ramp. The interior looked about as cozy as a steel coffin. He gave Jillian a side glance. "We shipping out immediately?"

She nodded, joining him inside. "Faster the better. Word is the outpost has gone full radio-silent. No calls. No signals."

She swallowed, and Ben saw a crack in her armor. *These were her friends. Not just colleagues.*

"We'll figure out what happened," he said softly.

CHAPTER 2

THEY TOOK off in the pre-dawn light, the plane's engines droning like a giant wasp. Ben settled into a seat by the window—if a porthole that small could be called a window—and tried to focus on the mission. He'd done a lot of weird gigs for the CSO, but a potential plague under the ice? That was new territory.

Across the aisle, Jillian pored over a thick binder of research notes. She scribbled in the margins, lips tight. Ben studied her for a moment, noting the tension in her posture. She looked young—maybe early thirties—yet carried a heavy load of responsibility. He guessed a few lines of worry on her face told enough of a story.

They had a refuel stop in Canada, then pushed on to Greenland. By the time they sighted the jagged coastline, the sky was a chalky gray, and the conversation had died into scattered attempts at small talk.

"You ever been to Greenland before?" Jillian asked, as Ben stared out at the white expanse.

He shook his head. "Nope. I try to only pick the tropical missions."

She attempted a weak smile. "That's probably wise."

The plane rattled through a patch of turbulence, and Ben gritted his teeth. "This seatbelt isn't exactly confidence-inspiring, but I guess it'll do."

A few hours later, they touched down at Kangerlussuaq Airport—one of the larger airstrips in Greenland. The surroundings looked like a lunar landscape dusted in white. Snow, rock, sky. Repeat. Temperatures bit at Ben's face the instant he stepped off the plane.

He was met by a tall, broad-shouldered man with a thick black beard. The man raised a hand in greeting. "Bennett?"

"That's me," Ben said, shifting his duffel to his other shoulder.

"Qannik," the man replied. "I guide. I drive. I fix broken stuff if it's not too broken."

Ben nodded, offered a quick handshake. Qannik had the look of a man who'd grown up here—comfortable in the cold, confident in his steps. Next to him stood a shorter man wrapped in a huge parka, who managed a curt nod. "Dr. Chuck Davis," he said. "I do the medical stuff. If you get shot or freeze a toe off, I'm your guy."

"Let's hope I don't need your services," Ben replied. He glanced around. "So how far is the station from here?"

Jillian came up behind him, pointing to a map on her phone. "We'll take a small plane from here to a rough airstrip the station uses. Then we'll do the rest by snowcat. Storm's coming in, so we need to hustle."

Ben sighed. *More planes, more frigid conditions. Great.* He'd sign up for a five-star beach resort in a heartbeat right now, but that wasn't exactly in the cards. "Lead the way."

The second flight was in a smaller two-prop plane, half cargo, half passenger seats. They crammed into the cabin with their gear. Their pilot Mara looked so relaxed that Ben envied her. She was flipping switches like she was operating a carnival ride.

A second later, he found out why. "This one's mine," she shouted over the engine noise. "I baby the hell out of her, too, since it's my livelihood."

He nodded.

"All strapped in back there?" she asked.

"Ready as we'll ever be," Ben replied, scanning the horizon. Clouds thickened overhead, promising a coming blizzard. Not ideal flying weather.

The plane jerked forward, gained speed on a short runway, and lifted into the sky. White tundra stretched in every direction, dotted with occasional dark ridges of rock. As they flew, Ben wondered what kind of operation the DoD had quietly funded. Infectious organisms under the ice? It sounded like the start of a bad horror movie.

He flicked a glance at Jillian. She stared out the window, brow furrowed. He tried to imagine what she was thinking—her colleagues were in trouble, quite possibly in mortal danger, and she'd had to leave them behind to seek help. She might be blaming herself, or the DoD, or both. CHECKPOOP: HOW DID SHE LEAVE/GET AWAY?

After about an hour, Mara dipped the plane's nose. "We're coming up on the station strip. Winds are getting nasty, though."

Ben's stomach flipped as the plane buffeted sideways. The seatbelt bit into his hips. He closed his eyes for a second, mentally cursing the job. If it wasn't viruses, it'd be high winds or bullet wounds. With the CSO, there was always a new thrill.

Finally, with a lurch, the plane touched down on a makeshift runway, bouncing over packed snow. The propellers coughed, engine whining down. When they rolled to a stop, Ben exhaled a breath he hadn't realized he was holding.

"Everyone intact?" Mara called. No one answered, which probably meant yes.

Outside, the storm's edge was hitting. Visibility dropped to maybe fifty yards, swirling flakes dancing in the wind. They transferred supplies to a hulking snow-cat, a massive tracked vehicle that looked like it had been built from a tank's spare parts. Qannik took the driver's seat, adjusting a pair of heavy goggles over his hat.

Ben and Jillian piled into the back with Dr. Davis. The interior smelled of oil and worn leather. There was a bench seat across from the cargo, which was mostly crates of medical gear, some rations, and a few rifles.

"Don't suppose we need the guns for polar bears?" Ben muttered.

Qannik overheard. "Depends on who else is at the station," he said, voice flat.

Ben tensed. "Wait, you think there might be—"

"I heard rumors. Other teams. Security contractors. Strange men paying visits," Qannik said. He shrugged a thick shoulder. "It's a remote place. People do odd things here."

Ben's mind flipped through possibilities. *Corporate saboteurs? Rival agencies? Or just paranoid rumors? Either way, best to be ready.*

The snowcat growled to life, treads crunching across the snow. They started forward at a steady pace, fighting the wind. Outside, the world was a whirl of white. Dr. Davis tapped a foot nervously. Jillian stared at a handheld GPS to keep them on track.

They traveled for an hour, maybe more—hard to tell in the featureless landscape. Conversation was minimal. Everyone seemed too keyed up, scanning for any sign of the station. Finally, a gray shape emerged through the storm.

"That's it," Jillian said, relief in her voice. "I think."

CHAPTER 3

QANNIK EASED the snowcat to a halt beside a metal building. A stenciled sign read: **GREENLAND CLIMATE RESEARCH – LARSEN FOUNDA-TION.** The place was eerily quiet. No lights in the windows. No one stepped out to greet them.

Ben unlatched the door and hopped down, boots sinking into drifting snow. Immediately, cold wind sliced across his face. He looked around. A few scattered outbuildings, a half-buried antenna tower. Tracks in the snow led away, but they were old, partially filled.

Jillian drew her hood tighter. "Power should be on. The generator can't just fail without someone noticing."

They trudged up to the main entrance, a steel door. Ben tried the handle. Locked. He exchanged a look with Jillian, who fished out a ring of keys. She tried two before the lock clicked.

Inside, the hallway was dark except for a flickering emergency light that tinted everything a sickly orange. The air was stale, with a faint metallic tang that put Ben on edge.

"Hello?" Jillian called, her voice echoing. "Anyone here?"

Silence.

They moved slowly, flashlights scanning left and right. Desks scattered with papers. A knocked-over chair. A half-eaten protein bar on a table, frozen solid. No people.

Ben's pulse sped up. If the team evacuated, they didn't do it neatly. If they were still here, they were hiding or...

He shook off the grim thought. *Focus.*

Dr. Davis stooped near a small patch of something on the floor. "This is blood," he said, shining his light. It was dried, dark brownish-red. "Not fresh, but not ancient either."

Ben grimaced. "So something went down."

Jillian looked paler than usual. "We need to check the labs."

In one corner of the building, they found a reinforced door labeled **LAB ACCESS**. Jillian's key worked here too, but the door stuck. It took both Ben and Qannik to yank it open, ice snapping around the frame.

A wave of cold, sterile air hit them. This area must have some partial power— Ben heard a faint hum from a backup system. They passed through a short corridor into a main lab space. Steel tables. Racks of instruments. The smell of chemicals and something else—something almost sweet, but off.

Ben nearly tripped over a sprawled figure on the floor. He crouched. A man in a lab coat, face hidden by a chunk of fallen debris. Dr. Davis knelt to check for vitals, but the man was stiff, eyes glazed. No saving him.

Then Ben saw the hole in his chest.

"He was shot," he said.

Jillian pressed a trembling hand to her mouth. "That's Dr. Werner Falk. Our lead glaciologist."

She was obviously struggling, but she kept it together. Ben knew exactly how she was feeling right now, and had to give her credit. This was not a woman used to seeing dead bodies — especially those of her friends and coworkers.

Let's just hope we don't find any more.

They searched for a sign of life, any life, among the scattered lab stations. Empty. Overturned chairs and scattered notebooks. A row of freezers hummed at the back, doors locked, lights flickering. One freezer door was wide open.

Jillian approached, peering inside. "This was supposed to house core samples," she whispered. "The older ones we pulled from deeper layers. It's empty."

Ben's breath plumed in the freezing air. "Did someone take them? Or trash them?"

She swore under her breath. "If the sample is gone, that means somebody wanted it. And if it's as dangerous as we think—"

"We're dealing with folks who have no clue what they've stolen," Dr. Davis finished.

"Or they know *exactly* what they've stolen," Ben added. He scanned the floor for more footprints or blood. "What about the other staff?"

Jillian looked around, eyes haunted. "We should check the secondary lab. There's a sub-level. Mostly used for storage. They might have holed up there."

They started toward a stairwell. That's when Ben heard it: a muffled scrape on the floor behind them. He whirled, flashlight beam sweeping across the door they'd come through. Something moved in the hallway. Slow. Deliberate.

Ben motioned for Qannik to dim the flashlight, and they crouched near a metal counter. Footsteps neared—heavy boots. More than one pair.

"Did you see anyone else outside?" he whispered.

Qannik and Jillian shook their heads.

Ben gritted his teeth. *Well, we're not alone.*

A moment later, he saw them through a gap in the doorframe: two men in thick parkas, rifles slung over their shoulders. They definitely weren't research staff. One had a face scar, the other a shaved head. They paused, talking in low voices. Ben couldn't catch the words, but it sounded like English.

They stepped into the lab. Scar-face grabbed a box from a shelf, rummaged through it, cursed softly. Shaved-head spat on the floor. Then they continued deeper into the building.

Ben exhaled quietly once they disappeared. "Mercenaries?"

Qannik's eyes narrowed as he nodded. "Not locals."

Jillian's whisper was barely audible. "They might have killed everyone for that sample."

Ben nodded. "But why hang around?"

Dr. Davis shrugged. "Could be a big payday waiting if they deliver the goods... or they're trying to gather more info."

Ben considered the options. Then he flicked his gaze to the back door. "We need to find out who's left alive. And if they jammed our comms, we have to fix that too."

They slipped out another corridor, hoping to avoid the armed men. The station's design was a warren of hallways and small labs. Eventually, Jillian found a hatch in the floor behind a stack of crates. She knelt and yanked it open, revealing a narrow ladder going down. The smell of stale air wafted up, tinged with an antiseptic odor.

Ben couldn't help but notice it would be a great hiding place — *and* a terrible escape route, if the men they'd seen chased them here.

Ben took point, climbing down. The space below was cramped, lined with shelves of old supplies—canned food, cleaning chemicals, extra lab equipment. One corridor led to a heavy door. A single emergency light flickered overhead.

Ben tested the door. Locked. He motioned Jillian forward with the ring of keys. She tried two. The third turned. The door squeaked open, revealing a sub-level lab area, smaller than the main one, with more freezers and sealed containers. It was a mess. Equipment in disarray, shelves knocked over.

Near the far wall, a young woman sat slumped against a toppled cabinet, hair matted with blood. She stirred as they approached, eyes fluttering open. "Jillian?" she rasped, disoriented.

Jillian rushed forward. "Ingrid? God, are you okay?"

Dr. Davis elbowed Ben aside, kneeling to check her. She had a nasty gash on her temple and looked severely dehydrated. "We need to get her out of here," he muttered.

Ingrid clutched Jillian's sleeve. "It was an accident. Stupid... mistake. I — I barely had any of the sample, and..."

She paused.

Jillian finished the sentence. "You were infected? With the virus?"

She nodded weakly. "Just... small dose. Any more than that and I'd be..."

Jillian shook her head, not needing Ingrid to continue. "What happened here?"

Ingrid swallowed, then answered. "They... took the sample." Her eyes rolled back, and she struggled to speak. "Falk tried to stop them, but... they shot him. Then took off."

Jillian glanced at Ben, horror in her eyes. "They're carrying around an infectious pathogen. One we have no idea how potent or deadly."

Ben pressed his lips together. *Great.* Armed mercenaries, potential carriers of an ancient virus, possibly on the loose. Could this day get better?

Dr. Davis checked Ingrid's pulse. "She's in shock. Let's get her upstairs, see if we can patch her up."

Ben nodded. He helped lift Ingrid gently. She managed a strained whisper: "Don't let them leave... unstoppable... if it gets out..."

CHAPTER 4

THEY BACKTRACKED TO THE LADDER, Ingrid cradled between Ben and Qannik. Suddenly, overhead, they heard shouting. Boots stomped across the floor. Something crashed, and a muffled voice cursed loudly.

Ben pushed to the side, into the corner of the room, pulling Qannik and Ingrid with him. Jillian put a finger to her lips, as she slipped next to Ben, all five bodies huddling in the darkest corner of the room, behind a stack of boxes, listening. Suddenly, the hatch above banged open. A flashlight beam probed the darkness, straight down the ladder and over the floor in front of it.

A mercenary peered down.

Ben's heartbeat thundered in his ears. They were caught if anyone made a sound. Ingrid was barely conscious, and he hoped she didn't groan or cough. Qannik looked ready to fight if it came to that.

The mercenary above squinted, trying to see. He muttered, "Might be nothing," then slammed the hatch shut.

Ben let out a silent breath. *That was too close.*

They waited another minute, and then he helped Qannik haul Ingrid up carefully. After they exited the hatch, they made a beeline for a side exit Jillian pointed to. Through that corridor, they found an alternate route to the outside—a maintenance door. Ben shoved it open, letting in a blast of freezing wind.

The snow outside was swirling even harder now, visibility maybe twenty yards at best. Their snowcat was on the far side of the main building. If they tried to get there, the mercenaries might spot them. But Ingrid needed real medical attention, and soon.

"What's the plan?" Dr. Davis hissed, teeth chattering. "We can't outrun them."

Ben surveyed the building's perimeter. "We slip around, keep low. Qannik, you scout ahead."

The big man nodded, took a few steps into the storm, and vanished behind drifting snow. Ben waited, listening for any sign of trouble. Moments later, Qannik reappeared, beckoning them forward. They moved as quietly as possible, Ingrid slung between Jillian and Dr. Davis, leaving Ben to scan the corners with a sidearm drawn.

As they neared the snowcat, Ben's spine tingled with tension, expecting a bullet to whiz by at any second. But none came. The mercenaries were probably still searching inside.

They bundled Ingrid into the snowcat's back seat. She moaned softly, half-unconscious. Dr. Davis rummaged for medical supplies. "I can stabilize her," he said, rummaging in the kit, "but she needs a full facility if that virus is in her system."

Ben slid into the passenger seat up front. "We can't just bail, though. Not if there's a chance these guys are about to waltz off with a doomsday bug."

Jillian leaned in from the back. "We might have an option. The station's radio tower is wrecked, but we have a backup dish about a mile from here. A relay station we used for data transmissions. If we can get there, maybe we can contact Mara for an immediate evac... or call in some bigger guns."

Ben stared at the swirling snow. "All right. Let's make for the relay. But keep an eye out. The mercenaries might have the same idea."

Qannik fired up the snowcat's engine, and they lumbered away from the station. Ben felt a pang of guilt, leaving behind the bodies of those scientists. But Ingrid was alive—and if they got out with her, maybe she and Jillian could still blow the whistle on this entire fiasco.

The snowcat moved at a crawl, fighting gusts of wind. The sky was a dull pewter overhead, with no break in the clouds. Ben's eyelids felt heavy. He'd been up for what, 24 hours now?

He glanced at Jillian. She was wide awake, eyes locked on Ingrid, who shivered in her seat, bundled in multiple jackets. A small part of Ben admired Jillian's courage: thrown into a crisis, colleagues dead or missing, possible plague on the loose, and she hadn't crumpled. She looked rattled, sure, but she kept going.

When the faint outline of a metal tower emerged from the haze, Ben's chest loosened in relief. They parked behind a drift and climbed out. The tower was about thirty feet tall, attached to a squat building half-buried in snow.

Jillian wasted no time, prying open the door to the building. Inside, equipment beeped softly in the glow of emergency lights. She rushed to a console, flipping switches. "If the generator's still functional, we can power the dish."

Ben hovered by the door, scanning outside with his flashlight. Qannik joined him, rifle slung. Dr. Davis settled Ingrid on a makeshift cot near the console, hooking her up to an IV. At least it was out of the wind.

Jillian tapped a button, cursing under her breath. "It's partially fried. But maybe I can send a narrow-band signal. Let me see..."

A burst of static crackled from a speaker. Then a faint beep. She leaned in, tried an emergency frequency. "Hello? Mara, do you copy? We need immediate evac. Come on..."

For agonizing seconds, the radio hissed. Then a voice, faint: "*—read you, but storm—too strong—need coordinates—*"

Relief flooded Jillian's face. "We have partial contact."

Ben tried not to grin. "Tell her to stand by. We might have to handle some housekeeping here before we can lift off."

Jillian's eyes flickered. "Housekeeping meaning... the mercenaries?"

Ben's jaw tightened. "We can't let them keep that sample. Not if it's as dangerous as you think."

A moment of silence. Even Dr. Davis paused from tending Ingrid, looking up. Qannik gave a solemn nod. "We have to go back."

"Qannik, you and I can go. Davis needs to keep an eye on. Ingrid, and Jillian can —"

"I'm going," she said quickly."

"The comms. Stay here and keep Mara in the loop. When we're ready for evac, you can be here."

"I can handle that," Dr. Davis said. "It's not like I'm doing surgery. Ingrid's stable, for now."

Jillian swallowed. "I need to go. Davis can try to get Mara to circle back in a short window. If she can find a break in the storm, she can pick us up. But we *have* to disable whoever's at the station. If they escape, the rest of the world's in deep trouble. I know the station, so I'll be able to help."

Ben turned to watch the snow swirl past the open doorway. He couldn't exactly argue. Jillian *was* the expert here. Still, the scale of the problem weighed on him.

Ancient virus, armed mercenaries, a potential mass outbreak.

Ben felt the fear and the thrill of stepping into the unknown. That was the CSO life—off-the-books problems with high stakes, relying on cunning, training, and a dash of luck.

And right now, he'd need all three.

CHAPTER 5

BEN SCANNED the pale glow of the radio console, watching Jillian's breath puff in the cold air. She looked both exhilarated and drained, like someone who'd sprinted a marathon only to realize she still had another mile to go. He stepped closer, rubbing his arms against the chill.

He could still hear the ragged breathing of Ingrid, lying on a makeshift cot in the corner. She was the only surviving scientist they'd managed to pull out of the station's sub-level. Dr. Davis crouched by her side, checking vitals, trying to keep her stable with the limited medical kit they'd hauled in. Qannik lingered near the door, flicking his gaze between the swirling snow outside and the overhead lights that pulsed in weak, unsteady flickers. No one said much. They all seemed to sense the next hammer was about to drop.

Jillian finally exhaled. "Got a partial signal out. Mara's on standby about a mile or two away, but with the storm this bad, she won't risk a landing unless there's a break."

Ben nodded grimly. "Might be the best we'll get. Meanwhile, the mercenaries are still at the station. If they get out of here with that virus sample, we can kiss any hope of containing this goodbye."

Jillian fiddled with the radio's frequency dial, frustration tightening her features. "They've already killed at least three of my colleagues, maybe more. Dr. Falk's body—" She trailed off, swallowing hard. The memory of finding him crumpled on the lab floor, dead for at least a day, would leave a bitter taste.

Ben glanced down at Ingrid. Her skin shone with sweat despite the freezing temperature, and her eyes fluttered as she drifted in and out of consciousness. Dr. Davis leaned in, speaking low, "She's not good. Whatever's in her bloodstream is causing a serious fever and delirium. Exposure hasn't helped. If that virus is in the mix, we're dealing with a wildcard."

Ben blew out a breath. "We don't have a choice. We go back and handle them. If we don't stop these guys, Ingrid won't be the only one dying from this thing."

Jillian stood taller, steeling herself. "How do you want to do it?"

Qannik shrugged in his quiet, no-nonsense way. "We sneak in, do what we have to. We already know some of the station's layout. We can hit them from a direction they won't expect."

Ben appreciated Qannik's calm approach—like he was reading from a checklist.

She inclined her head, tightening the hood on her coat. Her eyes flicked to Ingrid one last time. "Just remember, Dr. Falk was killed at least a day ago. That means the mercenaries first broke in back then. They're still lurking, probably because they realized there are *more* samples. Or maybe the storm pinned them down. Either way, they're rummaging for something else—data logs, research notes, extra vials. They might not have everything they need yet."

Ben bent over Ingrid, pressing two fingers gently to her shoulder. "Hang in there. We'll be back." He met Dr. Davis's gaze. "You sure you're okay holding down the fort?"

Davis nodded, though worry etched deeper into his face. "I'll keep her breathing. Just finish this."

They left the small relay building behind, locking the heavy door. The wind slammed them like a wall the moment they stepped out. Ice crystals pelted their coats and goggles, reducing the world to a swirl of white. The snowcat crouched nearby under a thickening drift, but they agreed it was too risky to drive—too loud, too likely to tip their hand.

So they went on foot, single file: Qannik at point, Jillian next, and Ben taking rear. Qannik navigated by subtle hints in the terrain—a shaped drift here, a wind-sculpted ridge there. If Ben tried to rely on his own sense of direction, he'd probably walk in circles. The storm made everything look the same.

He kept thinking about Dr. Falk's body in that lab, the hole in his chest. The mercs had left him like a piece of trash. *Why come back?* The only logical explanation was that they'd realized the station had more to offer: deeper core samples or digital research data. Possibly they couldn't exfil until the weather broke, so they were waiting for their own extraction.

It took them about forty minutes to approach the station in the near-blizzard. The structure loomed like a slab of shadow in the swirling white. Jillian motioned them around to a side entrance near the labs—the same route they'd used earlier, before rescuing Ingrid.

They forced the door open and slipped inside. The temperature difference was striking: still freezing, but calm, silent. The faint emergency lights tinted everything in a dull red glow. They crept down a hallway littered with scattered papers and broken lab gear—remnants of the mercs' first invasion.

Ben's mind flicked to Ingrid's half-conscious ramblings: *Don't let them leave... unstoppable... if it gets out...* He didn't see any obvious sign of the infected here. But if the virus had started spreading among the mercenaries, it might explain why they'd lost time, or why they were so desperate.

At an intersection, they paused. Blood smeared the floor—old enough to have dried, but not ancient. Ben swallowed the knot in his throat. "That's our turn down to the sub-level," he whispered, nodding to the right. "We already checked that area. If the mercenaries are here again, they might be searching the rest of the labs."

Jillian's gaze swept over the dark corridor. "They could also be trying to fix the jammed comms or salvage more data."

Qannik pointed left. "Dr. Falk's main office is that way. Computer banks. They might be hacking the logs."

They exchanged looks. Then they heard it: a clank from deeper down the left hallway, as if someone had knocked over a piece of equipment. Jillian mouthed, *Let's go.*

CHAPTER 6

THEY EASED FORWARD, guns raised. Ben could feel his pulse thrumming in his ears. Another lab door was cracked open, pale light slanting across the hall. He edged up and peeked through. Two mercenaries crouched over a row of shattered computer towers. One wore a scarf pulled up around his face; the other had a battered radio strapped to his vest. They were cursing at each other in hushed tones.

Ben's mind raced. *They must be looking for research data.* It was the only reason to fuss over old tower units. If the station's critical files were stored locally, these guys might assume there were more secrets to glean—maybe details on the virus or leads to the next lab.

He signaled Qannik and Jillian with quick hand motions: *two targets, center of the room.* Jillian drew a breath, then stepped around the corner, pistol leveled. Ben followed her lead, rifle aimed.

"Hands up," Jillian snapped.

The merc in the scarf jolted, scrambled for his sidearm. Ben fired a short burst into the floor near him—close enough to tear into his boot. The man yelped, dropping the gun. His partner grabbed for the radio, but Qannik advanced, aiming at his chest. The second merc froze.

For a beat, no one spoke, the tension so thick Ben could practically feel it. Then the merc with the scarf pressed a shaky hand to his bleeding foot. "Jesus— what do you want?"

Jillian kept her gun steady. "Answers. Why are you still here? You got the sample already."

The merc spat on the floor. "We took one set of vials, yeah. Found it in the freezers. But the doc—Falk—he had logs referencing something else. Another strain, deeper in the ice. We never found it."

Qannik gave Ben a knowing glance. They'd suspected the mercenaries were looking for more than a single sample. Possibly a mutated variant or a secondary data cache.

Ben jerked his head at the second merc. "Where's the rest of your team?"

The man glared but said nothing. Scarf-man winced, pressing a glove to his injured foot. "Gone. Some of them tried to bail when they realized how nasty this stuff was. The rest are still searching for anything valuable. Our boss wants to corner the market on 'doomsday viruses,' I guess." He gave an ugly, humorless chuckle. "Says we can name our price."

Jillian's face hardened. "That's insane. This thing could wipe out half the planet."

Scarf-man shrugged, eyes glinting with twisted greed. "Money's money. We're stuck anyway—the storm pinned us down. Might as well make the best of it."

Ben fought the urge to slam the guy's head into the console. Instead, he motioned at Qannik. "Check them for weapons."

Qannik deftly searched the men, tossing aside a pistol and a hunting knife. The second merc tried to spit at him, and Qannik elbowed him in the gut. He doubled over, wheezing.

Jillian pointed her pistol at scarf-man's chest. "Where's your boss?"

The man's lip curled. "He's in the sub-level again, or maybe the generator room. Keeps chasing rumors about a secondary stash." He grimaced. "You think I keep track of that psycho?"

Ben's gaze flicked to Jillian. If the boss was sniffing around the sub-level or generator area again, he might be nearing the deeper labs. "Tie these two up," he muttered. "We'll deal with them later."

It didn't take long to bind them with spare cable lying around. Qannik shoved them in a corner, out of reach of their weapons. Jillian grabbed a laptop they'd been fiddling with, scanning the screen. "They were ripping data onto a portable drive. It's about eighty percent done."

Ben's jaw tightened. If the mercs got away with that drive, they'd have everything the scientists worked on. Possibly the entire blueprint for weaponizing the virus. He yanked the USB stick out, ignoring the error message that flashed. "Not anymore."

Scarf-man let out a bark of protest. Jillian ignored him, snapping the laptop shut and stuffing it under her arm. "We can't let them keep any of this. I'll wipe the local backups when we're done."

Ben shouldered his rifle. "Then let's find the boss before he stumbles onto more samples."

Jillian pointed to the sub-level door. "We locked it up after we carried Ingrid out. They might've broken in again."

Ben led the way, Qannik at his flank, Jillian behind them. The door was indeed cracked open. Dim emergency lighting filtered through. Ben pressed his ear to the gap, listening. Footsteps echoed below, along with low voices. He heard a man bark an order, but he couldn't make out the words.

He turned to the others, and Jillian's expression said it all: *we end this now.*

CHAPTER 7

THEY LEFT the two mercs cursing in the lab, heading for the corridor. Every step they took, the station's old metal floors creaked, as if the building itself was on edge. They reached a T-junction leading toward the generator room on one side and the main sub-level stairwell on the other.

They descended slowly, rifles ready. The stairwell opened into the corridor where Ingrid had nearly died. Bloodstains on the floor had partially frozen. A few overhead bulbs flickered. Down at the far end, in front of the storage freezers, two figures rummaged through crates. One had his back turned, the other faced sideways.

The one turned sideways was tall, with a thin scar running from eyebrow to cheek. The other was hard at work on something, and Ben pegged him as the mercenaries' boss. He definitely carried himself like a man used to giving orders. A heavy sidearm was strapped to his thigh, and he had a radio in hand.

Ben turned off the safety on his rifle, lifted it, then took aim. Before he could speak or fire, the tall man's radio crackled. Someone up above was screaming about intruders, probably the two bound mercs from moments ago. The boss spun, and in that second, he locked eyes with Ben.

Shouting erupted. Qannik fired first, catching the second merc in the shoulder. Jillian ducked behind a half-shattered supply crate, letting off two shots that hammered the wall inches from the boss's head. He lunged sideways, returning fire with precise, controlled bursts. Bullets sparked off the metal floor near Ben's feet. Ben dropped to a knee, steadied, and fired a triple tap. One round grazed the boss's upper arm. The man cursed and dove behind a large freezer canister.

Ben's heart pounded, the acrid smell of gunpowder mixing with the station's stale air. He darted a look at Jillian. She was reloading, jaw clenched in concentration. Qannik moved with lethal calm, edging around crates to flank their opponents.

The second merc, wounded and in a panic, tried to raise his rifle again. Qannik put him down with a single shot. The man crumpled to the floor. That left the boss pinned behind the freezer.

Jillian pressed against the opposite side of the freezer, glancing at Ben. "He's cornered," she mouthed.

But the boss was no amateur. He popped up, gun blazing, forcing Jillian to retreat with a startled cry. Then he made a break for the back door—an emergency exit that led to a smaller cargo elevator. Ben lunged after him, ignoring the burn in his lungs from the cold. He caught a glimpse of the boss's coat vanishing through the door.

Jillian and Qannik rushed up behind Ben. The door slammed shut, a manual bolt lock clicked. Ben threw his shoulder into it, but it held. He heard the metallic groan of the cargo elevator powering up beyond. If the boss managed to ascend and slip out onto the ice, he might vanish into the storm with any vials he still had.

"Stand back," Qannik snapped, raising his rifle at the lock. One short, sharp blast. The lock shattered, the door swung open. They barreled through into a cramped elevator bay. A chain-link gate halfway across the elevator shaft rattled as it lifted, the boss inside holding some sort of case in one hand, his gun in the other, frantically pressing the control panel to ascend. He fired a few blind shots downward. One whizzed past Jillian, skipping off the concrete floor.

Ben gritted his teeth, aimed high, and squeezed the trigger. The bullet snapped through the chain-link, grazing the boss's leg. The man howled, stumbling sideways. But the elevator kept rising. Another second, and he'd be out of reach.

Jillian sprinted forward, slamming the emergency stop button on a nearby control box. Sparks flew, and the elevator jerked to a halt about eight feet off the ground—just high enough to leave the boss exposed. Qannik fired twice, each round punching through the chain-link. The boss dropped to his knees with a strangled cry, gun clattering.

Ben and Jillian rushed to the base of the elevator. The man lay on the floor of the cage, clutching a black container that looked suspiciously like the ones in the storage labs. Ben's stomach turned. *That might be it—the virus.*

Jillian lifted her pistol, eyes dark with anger. "Drop it."

The boss's lips curled in a sneer of pain and defiance. He let go of the container and raised bloody hands. "Go ahead and shoot," he spat. "You have no idea what you're dealing with."

Ben let out a harsh breath. "We know enough. You stole something that could kill millions."

"Only if it's used wrong," the boss hissed, blood dripping from his mouth.

"We... we have labs. We can refine it, sell it. People pay a fortune for this. You wouldn't believe the—"

Jillian fired a single shot that smacked the metal floor an inch from his arm. The boss flinched violently. "Shut up. We're done listening."

Ben carefully reached through the chain-link, gripping the container handle. The boss tried to lunge for it, but Qannik shoved the muzzle of his rifle under the man's chin. That ended any argument.

Ben tugged the container free. It felt cold and ominous in his hands, like it was humming with malevolence. Jillian pressed the stop button again, releasing the elevator's lock. It lurched, dropping back down to floor level with a squeal.

Qannik yanked the boss out and forced him face-down onto the ground, binding his wrists with a length of cord. Blood slicked the floor around them, but the man was still alive, panting curses under his breath.

Jillian bent over the container, flicking the latch. Inside, test tubes and vials nestled in foam, each labeled with coded designations. Her expression was grim. "This is definitely more of Dr. Falk's stash. I don't recognize most of these, which tells me it's the project he's been working on — the one the DoD had him focused on. Maybe even variations on the virus. We have to keep it sealed."

Ben's adrenaline finally began to subside, leaving him shaking and numb. He exchanged a look with Qannik, who nodded once, acknowledging victory—or at least the closest thing to it in this nightmare.

They had the boss, they had the samples, and the storm still raged outside. But now, if Mara could find a gap in the weather, they might actually lock this down.

Ben exhaled, pulling the container tight against his chest. "Let's get back to Ingrid and Dr. Davis, call Mara. And let's make sure these bastards can't do this again."

Jillian nodded, stepping aside so Qannik could march the wounded boss forward. "One problem at a time. But at least we got them—and we got this." She gently tapped the container.

They turned, leading their prisoner back through the station, leaving behind the echoes of a dead man's dream for profit and power. Despite the howling storm, for the first time in hours, Ben felt like they had a fighting chance.

CHAPTER 8

BEN LED the way back through the bowels of the station, clutching that black container of samples under one arm. Behind him, Jillian walked with her pistol drawn, while Qannik guarded the mercenary boss, forcing the wounded man forward at a steady clip. The boss gritted his teeth, one leg trailing blood, but managed a staggering march. His curses and mutterings under his breath only stopped when Qannik prodded him in the back with the muzzle of his rifle.

Every corridor they passed looked more sinister in the dying light. The air felt colder, too. Ben wondered if the backup generator was finally giving up. Usually, in a place like this, the temperature was artificially maintained just above freezing. Now, the chill crept in from every corner, like the entire station was surrendering to the polar night.

As they neared the stairs up from the sub-level, Ben's ears strained for any noises. No more gunfire. No pounding footsteps. The ones who were still alive might be hiding or have fled. He thought of the pair they'd tied up in Dr. Falk's old office—still alive, presumably. They'd have to deal with them, but the biggest threat was the boss.

Jillian's lips thinned as she climbed the stairs. Her breath rattled in short, frosty puffs, her arms clasped around the laptop as they moved. They emerged into the corridor near the main lab—a familiar sight. Dr. Falk's body was still there, dead and frozen. Ben swallowed hard. At least they'd be able to identify him. Maybe that would give Jillian and Ingrid some sense of closure, if that was even possible.

The mercenary boss staggered, letting out a low groan. "You're making a mistake," he rasped.

Ben didn't humor him with a reply. He just kept the container pinned tight to his ribs. That was the lynchpin here. All the data, all the horror, revolved around these vials. If they lost them now, it was game over for everyone.

Jillian finally spoke as they turned a corner. "You killed an entire research station for 'market share.' Or was that just your interpretation of the plan?"

The boss exhaled a bitter laugh. "You'd be surprised how valuable a doomsday cure can be. Or how profitable the threat of a new disease could become for the right buyer. Governments pay top dollar to get ahead of a potential plague."

Ben's fists clenched. He kept going, not giving the man the satisfaction of a reaction. But that last line hammered home the twisted logic behind these mercs. With Dr. Falk's data and a living, ancient virus, they could blackmail or sell to the highest bidder.

Classic extortion on a global scale.

They found the two bound mercenaries where they'd left them, in the makeshift computer lab near the broken towers. One had managed to wiggle free enough to shift the cable around his ankles, but he still sat trapped in a corner. He froze when he saw Ben and Qannik dragging in the boss. The other looked wild-eyed, clearly not expecting their leader to get hauled back under guard.

Jillian marched over to the battered computer desk, hunting for anything else the mercs might have stolen. She found a small flash drive, half-hidden under a tangle of wires. She pocketed it, ignoring the two captives as they spat insults at her. One demanded medical help for his shot-up foot. Jillian ignored that too.

Ben glanced around the wrecked lab, mind clicking through the next steps. "We'll lock these guys together in one place. The storm's not letting up, so it's not like they can run out into the blizzard. Then we get the hell back to the relay station."

Qannik poked the boss in the ribs. "You heard him. Move."

The boss dropped onto a metal bench near his lackeys, hissing in pain when his wounded leg bent. The other two mercs glared at him, maybe shocked to see him captured. One started to open his mouth with a question, but Qannik cut him off with a grunt. In short order, they had all three bound up together with cable and ripped strips of leftover canvas from a lab tarp.

Jillian took a step back, pressing a hand to her chest as if trying to steady her heart. "Should we search the station for more stragglers?" she asked, voice low.

Ben considered the possibility. They'd already dealt with or discovered these guys. But he wasn't sure if it was the only mercenary group that had come through here. That implied that some could have fled or died. A few might still be lurking—wounded or stranded. "We'll do a quick sweep," he decided. "Make sure no one's left to ambush us. Then we're out."

He turned to the prisoners. "Where's the rest of your team?"

One of the bound mercs kicked at the floor. "Let me out, and I'll tell you whatever you want to know."

Ben slid the container onto a nearby desk, resting his rifle on his shoulder. "Any chance there are others who may have tried to get out the main entrance?"

The merc gave a sneer. "Have fun checking. You'll freeze to death before you find 'em."

Ben ignored that. "Qannik, stay here, keep an eye on them. Jillian and I will do a fast loop around the upper level."

Qannik nodded. "Don't take too long."

Ben lifted the virus container again, then paused. Leaving it near these guys felt like a bad idea, no matter how securely they were tied up. He patted it once, as if verifying it was real. "I'll keep it with me," he decided, shifting the weight to his off-hand. "Just in case."

He and Jillian slipped back into the corridor. A hush settled over them. Distantly, the wind pounded the station walls. Some of the overhead lights had finally gone dark, leaving entire hallways in near-blackness. Ben's flashlight roved over battered doors and broken windows. The place felt emptier than before.

They peered into each major room in turn. Mostly carnage and abandoned equipment. One lab had bullet-riddled monitors. Another had a row of freezers, their doors ajar. Ben noticed frost building up inside, creeping over the metal racks. If these had any leftover samples, they were probably worthless now—thawed, refrozen, partially destroyed. Or the mercs had taken them. Hard to tell which was worse.

When they reached the main entrance at last, they saw the door wide open to a swirl of snow. Drifts had blown in, dusting the floor with a thin layer of white. A shattered side window rattled in the gale. Jillian shone her flashlight around, revealing footprints that led outside and vanished.

It could have been mercs, or it could have been one of the station staff, though that seemed less likely given the older footprints.

She stepped to the threshold, peering out. The storm beyond looked vicious, snow flying sideways. The sky was a dark slate, no sign of dawn or dusk. She shook her head, pulling back from the onslaught. "If anyone ran that way, they're probably not surviving long."

Ben let out a slow breath. He tried to picture someone deciding that braving minus-whatever-degree temperatures in a blizzard was better than staying in the station.

Might be insane... or just desperate.

CHAPTER 9

HE GENTLY SHUT the outer door. The latch was broken, so it didn't lock, but at least it cut off some of the wind. "We've seen enough. Let's get back to Qannik and head for the relay."

They retraced their steps. Jillian's voice stayed tight with worry. "What if the power fails completely there? The backup generator's got to be almost out of diesel. If the relay station's heat goes, there's no telling what'll happen to Ingrid's chances of getting well, or how the virus might degrade."

Ben's gaze flicked to the container in his arms. "We should hope it degrades, right?"

She shook her head. "Maybe. But if it's stable enough, a partial freeze won't kill it. And if some mutated strain survived at deeper levels, we don't know what temperature range it can handle."

He felt a chill that had nothing to do with the subzero air. "Then we keep it locked up, ship it out to a secure facility. Let the real experts figure out disposal—assuming we can trust them."

Jillian sighed. "One crisis at a time. Right now, that means leaving before the weather pins us in too."

They circled back to the room where Qannik guarded the prisoners. He stood with arms folded, staring at them as if daring one of them to try something. The boss was slumped against the wall, breathing heavily, a sheen of sweat on his face. The other two glowered in sullen silence.

Ben jerked a thumb at the hall. "We're clear. No one else left on this floor, unless they're hiding under a desk. Let's pack up."

Qannik gave a short nod. "Good. Let's get them out of here."

Ben paused. What to do with the prisoners? They couldn't drag them through the storm. Dr. Davis certainly couldn't handle that many wounded men.

And if Mara landed, they couldn't fit everyone on a small plane anyway. Not with limited seats and space.

Jillian voiced the conundrum. "We could lock them in one of the labs, but there's no guarantee they'll survive. Or we could leave them with a radio, let them call for help once we're gone."

Ben studied the three men, thinking how many people they'd murdered. Then again, they were no good to him dead. "We're not executioners," he said quietly. "We'll lock them up tight, leave a note for search-and-rescue, or the local authorities. Let them deal with the consequences of a break-in like this."

The boss bared his teeth in a savage grin. "We'll get out eventually."

Ben set the sample container on a table. He forced a calm he didn't quite feel. "Maybe you will. But by then, we'll be long gone. And this—" He tapped the container. "—is staying out of your hands."

The boss's grin faded, replaced by a glare of raw hatred. He said nothing more.

They moved the men, under Qannik's watch, to a secure storage closet with metal walls and a sturdy inner latch. The boss snarled when they shoved him inside, but he didn't resist beyond a few curse words. The wounded merc who'd been shot in the foot gritted his teeth, hissing in pain with every step. Once they were all locked in, Jillian jimmied the handle from outside, then used a coil of chain and a padlock from a broken toolbox to reinforce it. It wouldn't hold forever, but hopefully it'd hold long enough.

Ben scrounged up a half-full jug of water and some energy bars from a supply shelf. He opened the closet door a crack, shoved them inside, then slammed it again. "So you can't say we didn't offer anything," he muttered.

A sour stench of blood and sweat clung to the hall. Ben swallowed down the tension in his throat. He hefted the container once more. "Let's go. Before we freeze solid."

They trudged out of the station the same way they'd come, through the side corridor that led to the battered exit. The storm's fury hadn't lessened; if anything, it felt stronger. Snow scoured their faces as soon as they stepped outside. Visibility was close to zero. Qannik huddled near Jillian, making sure neither of them lost sight of Ben in the whiteout. For a moment, Ben imagined the mercenaries locked inside that station, pacing the room, waiting for rescue that might never come.

He suppressed the flicker of pity. They'd made their choices.

Their trip back to the relay station felt even longer, the wind forcing them to lean forward at a precarious angle. Once, Jillian stumbled into a waist-deep drift, nearly losing her footing entirely. Ben grabbed her arm, hauled her upright. She gave him a shaky nod of thanks, eyes wide with adrenaline.

All the while, Ben clutched the briefcase container like it was his own personal shield against the storm—and the madness. Each step he took, the weight of the vials inside pressed on him, a constant reminder that the job was only half-finished. Ingrid was still fighting for her life, and they still had to get out of Greenland in one piece.

When the faint outline of the relay building came into view, relief rushed through him. The dish antenna jutted from the roof at a crooked angle, battered by the gale, but still standing. They stumbled to the door, hammered three times.

Dr. Davis unlatched it from the inside. He blinked at them, relief etched onto his face. "Thank God. Ingrid's getting worse. Fever spiked about ten minutes ago."

They piled in, slamming the door behind them, panting as the warmth—or what little warmth there was—enveloped them. Ben set the container carefully on a counter, like an offering at an altar. Jillian rubbed her numbed cheeks, flinching when she touched raw skin. Qannik brushed the snow off his shoulders.

Davis ushered them toward Ingrid. She lay limp, hair plastered to her brow with sweat, eyes half-lidded. Her breathing was shallow, rasping. Davis glanced at them anxiously. "Did you find any medication? Anything that could help?"

Jillian bit her lip. "We, uh... we found what the mercenaries took. Got a laptop and some data. But not medical supplies. The place is trashed. We'll have to rely on what you've got in here, Doc."

He nodded grimly, then sighed. "I've done all I can. She needs a hospital, or at least a real infirmary. Something to bring the fever down."

Ben sighed, tilting his head toward the radio console. "Any luck contacting Mara?"

CHAPTER 10

DAVIS HURRIED OVER, flipping a switch. White noise hissed through the small speaker. He turned the dial, and a sudden burst of static turned into a distant voice: Mara, calling from overhead, fighting the wind. *"—you read me? Storm's not clearing enough to land safely... might have one shot at a rough approach near the relay... but the skis on this plane—"*

Her words cut out in a buzz. Jillian raced over and snatched the mic. "Mara, it's Jillian. If you can find a patch of flat ice near here, we can come to you. Ingrid can't wait much longer."

Silence for a few agonizing seconds. Then Mara's voice crackled back in. *"Copy. — see a shallow basin about three hundred —north of your building. The wind's borderline... I can try it once."*

Ben felt a surge of hope. "We'll be there," he muttered, mostly to himself. Then into the mic, "We have one who needs a real medical facility, stat."

Jillian quickly explained about Ingrid's condition, the virus sample, and the urgent need for exfil. Mara sounded rattled but resolute. *"Roger that. I'll circle back in twenty minutes. Be ready. If I can't land, I'll have to wave off and come back tomorrow—assuming the storm breaks."*

Tomorrow was too late. They all knew it. Ingrid might not last that long, and neither would the minimal generator power in this battered outpost. Without even the feeble amount of heat in here, hypothermia would set in well before tomorrow.

Ben locked eyes with Jillian, then with Qannik. "We're loading Ingrid and the sample onto that plane, no matter what it takes."

Davis began packing up a portable med kit, hooking Ingrid to a small IV bag. Qannik and Ben improvised a stretcher from spare boards and blankets. Jillian rummaged for anything else they might need: flares, rope, hand warmers. The last was humorous to Ben; if they did get stuck somewhere, at least the hand warmers would keep them alive for approximately seven minutes longer. She paused to look over the battered screens of the relay's computer, checking once more for any sign that the mercs might have jammed them again.

She gave Ben a look: *everything seems normal.*

In ten minutes, they were as ready as they could be. Davis and Qannik carefully lifted Ingrid onto the makeshift stretcher, bundling her in coats and scarves to keep her from freezing mid-transit. She moaned, eyes half-open, but didn't protest. Ben slung the virus container across his shoulder, secured by a strap. Jillian grabbed the radio gear, looping it around her torso.

The moment they opened the door, the storm ripped at them again. Their small band emerged, blinking against the driving snow. The cold gnawed at every inch of exposed skin. With Ingrid's stretcher between them, Davis and Qannik moved in unison, step by step, bracing for each sudden gust. Jillian trailed beside them, calling out directions from a half-working GPS, trying to pinpoint that shallow basin Mara had mentioned.

Ben took the lead, scanning the void. Once more, they walked single file, though this time the trek felt more urgent, more precarious. Ingrid's life literally hung in the balance. Under his arm, the virus container bumped with each step, a constant reminder of the other threat waiting to be unleashed if they failed.

They trudged for what felt like hours but was probably only fifteen minutes. At one point, the wind let up just enough for Ben to see a patch of relatively level snow ahead. He thought he spotted the faint shape of an aircraft's lights descending in a wide arc. "That has to be Mara," he shouted over his shoulder, voice yanked away by the wind.

Sure enough, the roar of an engine approached. A small, twin-prop plane skimmed through the swirling darkness, landing skis scraping the ice in a shower of snow. It bucked and swayed as Mara fought for control, eventually sliding to a halt maybe fifty yards ahead of them.

Ben felt a wave of relief so sudden it made him lightheaded. "Go!" he yelled. They pressed forward, Ingrid's stretcher bobbing. The plane's engines revved, the pilot apparently keeping them hot in case the storm worsened. Mara flung open a side hatch, waving frantically. Her face was nearly invisible behind goggles and a thick scarf, but Ben recognized her no-nonsense posture.

They hustled Ingrid inside first. Dr. Davis followed, situating her across a row of seats that had been removed to make space. Qannik climbed after, passing in supplies. The plane rocked in the wind, threatening to tilt.

Jillian half-fell into the cabin, snow shaking off her as she entered. Ben was last, struggling to get the container through the narrow hatch. The wind caught him like a fist, and for a moment he nearly lost his footing. Qannik reached out, grabbed his arm, and hauled him in. He collapsed onto the floor, chest heaving, the container pressed to his side. Mara slammed the hatch behind them.

He looked up at her, breathless. "We got it," he wheezed. "Hopefully it's enough."

Mara jerked a thumb at the cockpit. "Strap in. This is going to be rough."

They had no time to ask questions. The engines revved, the plane pivoted, and Mara gunned it, skis scraping over ice. Outside, the visibility was near-zero, but she aimed for whatever gap in the storm she'd spotted from the sky. A deafening roar filled the cabin, drowning out Ingrid's delirious moans. Ben gripped the wall, heart hammering.

Jillian wrestled with her harness, face pale. Davis hovered over Ingrid, shouting instructions to Qannik about holding the IV bag steady.

Then the plane lurched up, bouncing in the wind. The landing skis left the ground. For a terrifying second, it felt like they'd get slammed back down. But Mara coaxed the aircraft upward, fighting the gale. They jerked side to side, climbing slowly. Ben's stomach churned.

A loud — and not very reassuring sounding — beeping came from somewhere in the cockpit. Another gust struck them, sending the plane tilting. Mara cursed. Then at last, they were through the worst of it, leveling out into a higher altitude, above the swirling madness.

No one spoke for a solid minute, too busy gulping for air and trying to calm racing hearts. When they finally did, Jillian looked at Ben, her voice raspy. "That was... insane."

He couldn't disagree. The container still dug into his side, reminding him of how precarious this victory was. Ingrid was alive, but for how long if they didn't get her to a real hospital? And what about the battered station with mercenaries locked inside?

Mara glanced back from the cockpit. "We're flying blind until we clear the storm's edge. Once I can get a stable bearing, I'll take us to Kangerlussuaq Airport. If their runway's iced over, we might have to divert. Either way, doc, get ready."

Dr. Davis nodded, wiping sweat from his brow. "I just hope Ingrid holds out."

Ben gently patted Ingrid's shoulder. She stared at him through half-lidded eyes, maybe recognizing him, maybe not. He leaned back, finally letting the exhaustion seep through his muscles. They had the sample. The mercs were disarmed or dead. Ingrid had a fighting chance.

He tried to find some relief in that, but his mind kept returning to the violence they'd left behind. To Dr. Falk's body. To the research logs that might still exist on some hidden drive.

The plane rattled through another gust. Ben closed his eyes. For now, at least, they were alive, Ingrid was breathing, and the virus was contained. He'd take that as a win—even if the real fallout was only just beginning.

CHAPTER 11

BEN FELT the plane jolt again as Mara fought against a turbulence pocket. She didn't coddle the aircraft—she wrestled it, every movement purposeful, every muscle tense. He glanced at the others. Jillian had her eyes shut, lips pressed together in a tight line. Qannik gazed out the little window, expression set, as if he were willing the plane to stay airborne by sheer force of will. Dr. Davis hovered over Ingrid, checking her breathing, adjusting the IV line. Ingrid remained half-conscious, her skin clammy, eyes unfocused.

Ben tried to block out the roar of the engines and the whine of the wind. He focused on the container strapped to his side—on the vials inside. Part of him wanted to fling it out the door, into the icy void, just to be done with it. But if destroying the virus was that simple, Dr. Falk and his team would have done it themselves. For all Ben knew, the pathogen might survive sub-zero freefalls and come back twice as nasty. They needed a secure lab, a real facility. Somewhere with blast-proof walls and thick steel doors.

He breathed in slowly, counting to three, letting the plane's vibrations lull him into a mechanical sort of calm. Jillian caught his eye. She mouthed something like *We're okay*. He nodded. They both knew that was only partly true.

Mara's voice crackled through the cabin intercom. "There's a lull forming on the approach to Kangerlussuaq. I'm heading for it, but this is going to be bumpy."

Ben unbuckled himself, just enough to scoot closer to Ingrid and Dr. Davis. "How's she holding up?"

Davis didn't look up. "Fever's still spiking. She's close to delirious again. I'm worried about septic shock." He tapped a penlight against Ingrid's pupils, checking her responses. "We need a hospital, now."

Ben frowned. "Hang on to her a little longer. We're almost there."

The plane tipped forward in a controlled descent. By the time the runway lights flickered into view, evening had settled—a dark, swirling gloom across the horizon. The snowstorm's edge was still raging to the west, but if Mara could ride the boundary just right, they might pull this off. Ben gritted his teeth, bracing for impact as Mara dropped lower.

They touched down with a nail-rattling screech of skis against ice and tarmac. The plane skidded, yawing sideways. For a terrifying moment, Ben thought they'd spin out. Mara wrestled the controls, the engines roaring, until the plane straightened and slid to a stop. Adrenaline crashed through his veins. He hadn't realized he was holding his breath until Qannik clapped a hand on his shoulder.

"We made it," Qannik said in a low voice, like he was almost surprised.

Jillian pulled the hatch open as soon as Mara killed the engines. A blast of frigid air rushed in, but it was nowhere near as brutal as the interior ice sheet had been. Here, the wind was strong but not catastrophic. Through the open hatch, Ben saw the faint lights of a small control tower and a few squat buildings. A pair of bundled-up figures hurried out from one structure, carrying a stretcher.

Mara unbuckled and stepped into the cabin, shaking out her arms. "Folks here radioed they've got a small med facility on-site—more of a clinic, really. Better than nothing."

Ben had never been so relieved to see a makeshift airport in his life. Davis and Qannik carefully hauled Ingrid out, passing her to the waiting ground crew. One was an older Greenlandic nurse wearing a heavy parka, and the other a wiry man who might have been the airfield's manager. They guided Ingrid onto a proper hospital stretcher, wheeling her toward a nearby building that probably doubled as both security office and medical station.

Jillian hopped down next, nearly stumbling when her boots hit the icy tarmac. Ben landed beside her, holding the virus container tight. His shoulders ached from the tension of the flight, but he forced himself to stand tall. "Let's go with her," he said.

They hurried after the stretcher, heads bowed against the wind. The lights from the building glowed in a dull orange, reminding him of the emergency lamps back in the station. At least here, there were four sturdy walls and some rudimentary heaters.

Inside, the difference was immediate—warmer by a few precious degrees, the hum of a generator in the background. The floors were scuffed linoleum, the walls old cinder blocks with posters in Danish and English about arctic safety. The nurse directed them down a short corridor into a cramped exam room. Dr. Davis laid Ingrid on a narrow cot with help from Qannik, while the local man fussed with a wall-mounted medical kit.

Jillian stood near the door, hair disheveled and face still flushed from the cold. Her eyes flicked to Ben. "Think we can trust them?" she whispered, worry etched in her features.

Ben's gaze drifted to Ingrid's pale face. "Got no choice. At least they have better supplies than we had."

Davis was already barking instructions. "She's got possible systemic infection, extremely high fever. I need IV antibiotics, cooling measures. Now."

The nurse hustled to a supply cabinet, rummaging for the medication. Ben took a half step backward, letting the professionals do their work. The tiny room felt jammed with people and gear. He clutched the container at his side, aware that the vials within might be more lethal than any bullet or scalpel.

Qannik tapped him on the shoulder, leaning in close. "What about the authorities? You planning to call them in, or do we just vanish?"

Ben chewed the inside of his cheek. "We can't vanish. The moment Ingrid gets stable, we need to coordinate a real rescue for the station. The mercenaries are locked up, but that won't hold forever."

Qannik nodded. "And we have your cargo." He flicked a glance at the container. "Someone will want that. Government, military, corporate big shots... Doesn't matter who—it'll be trouble."

Ben exhaled a long breath. "It's a can of worms, that's for sure. But if we keep it quiet for now, maybe we can pass it off to a legit lab or to the authorities who won't try to weaponize it."

Jillian stepped closer, overhearing. Her face was lined with fatigue. "We need an official chain of custody, or we risk it slipping into the wrong hands. CSO has connections, right?"

"Yeah," Ben said, thinking about his brief conversation with the man named Chambers. Ben would just make this his problem, as soon as possible. "We'll keep it under wraps until we figure out the next step. Right now, Ingrid's survival comes first."

At the cot, Dr. Davis was already hooking Ingrid up to an IV drip and an oxygen canister. The local nurse fumbled with bandages and a digital thermometer, muttering in Danish under her breath. Davis waved a hand at Ben. "We might have to get her to a proper hospital in Nuuk or even Reykjavik if her fever doesn't break. It's risky flying, though."

A shaky voice rose from the cot. Ingrid's eyes were open, dull but aware. "Ben?" she whispered, the syllable clipped by a hoarse cough. "Did you... get the sample?"

He stepped to her side, holding up the black container so she could see. "We got it. It's safe. We're not letting it out of our sight."

Relief flickered in her expression, then pain twisted her features again. "Don't... don't let them study it. They'll want it for... the wrong reasons." She drifted off, eyelids fluttering.

Ben set a hand gently on her shoulder. "Easy. We'll handle it. You just worry about getting better."

She didn't respond, already slipping back into a feverish half-sleep. Dr. Davis frowned, feeling her pulse. "Her temperature is still climbing. We need more advanced resources." He spoke to the nurse in a slow, measured tone, confirming they had the right antibiotics. The nurse nodded and prepped an injection.

Jillian backed away, rummaging through her pockets for her phone. Her gloved fingers fumbled, and she shot Qannik a frustrated look. "Signal here is spotty, but I might be able to get a message out to the main airport ops. They can route a request for an air ambulance, or a Coast Guard helicopter."

Ben took the opportunity to check in with Mara, who was presumably still outside prepping the plane for refueling or safety protocols. He left the exam room and followed a short hallway that ended in a small waiting area. Everything smelled of disinfectant and stale coffee.

He spotted Mara through a window. She was chatting with an airport worker, arms gesturing wildly—likely describing their insane landing. Ben tapped on the glass, got her attention. She nodded once, as if to say *Working on it,* then turned back to the worker. With any luck, they'd figure out how to refuel or how best to keep the plane here while the storm battered the rest of the island.

CHAPTER 12

HE RETURNED to the exam room to find Qannik standing guard near the door, arms folded. Jillian was off to the side, phone pressed to her ear, trying to get a call through. Ingrid lay motionless on the cot, hooked up to tubes and sensors, while Dr. Davis and the nurse worked in hushed concentration.

Ben set the container down on a table near the wall, never taking his eyes off it for more than a second. He didn't see many official-looking faces around—no uniformed police or military. Maybe that was a blessing. They could keep a low profile for the moment.

Jillian lowered her phone with a half grin. "Got a call through to the capital. They said they'll try to scramble a chopper to take Ingrid to a bigger hospital, weather permitting. Might not be until morning, but it's something."

Ben nodded, tension easing an inch. "Good. We can keep her alive 'til then, hopefully."

Qannik shifted his weight. "And the mercenaries at the station?"

Ben rubbed the back of his neck. "We'll let the Greenlandic authorities know. They can coordinate a rescue or a bust, whichever it turns into. If it takes them a day or two to get out there, those guys might have to get cozy with each other. But I'm not losing any sleep over that."

He moved to the small window in the exam room, peering out at the snow swirling under the floodlights. The storm's edge still raged in the distance, but here, at least, they had relative calm.

Jillian came up beside him, slipping her phone away. She spoke softly, mindful of Ingrid's labored breathing behind them. "We did it, Ben."

He let out a quiet laugh that held no real humor. "Yeah. We did. Doesn't feel like a celebration. So many people died back there."

Her expression darkened. "I know. But Falk would have wanted that virus contained. I'm sure of it."

Ben looked down at his gloves, which were torn and bloodstained from the scuffle in the station. "We just need to make sure no one else tries to weaponize it. Or replicate it. Or sell it." He glanced at the container, a surge of fierce protectiveness rising in him. "We saw what happened to the mercs who meddled with it."

Jillian gave a small nod, exhaustion in every line of her face. "One step at a time. We'll get Ingrid stable, then figure out who to call, who to trust."

He didn't mention the possibility of the CSO stepping in more formally—that phone call would come soon enough. For now, they were just a handful of people who'd made it out alive, carrying the sort of secret that could topple governments if played wrong.

"Doc," Qannik said, breaking the hush. He nodded at Dr. Davis, who was finishing an injection. "How's she doing?"

Davis stood, rolling his stiff shoulders. "Better oxygen saturation than before, but the fever's still insane. This antibiotic should help if it's a standard infection. If it's that ancient virus? That's a crapshoot. We'll see."

The nurse murmured something in Greenlandic, offering a sympathetic expression. Davis translated. "She says we should rest in shifts, in case Ingrid deteriorates or if we need to help with the generator."

Ben nodded. That sounded like good advice. The adrenaline had ebbed, and a leaden fatigue weighed on him. They arranged themselves as best they could—Qannik found a folding chair near the corridor, Jillian settled against a wall with her knees drawn up, and Ben perched on a stiff stool by Ingrid's side, the virus container at his feet.

He tried to stay awake, to keep watch, but the constant hum of the heater and the low hush of conversation tugged him under. A few minutes of sleep, that was all he needed. Just enough to gather strength for whatever came next.

His eyes drifted shut.

He woke an hour or two later—hard to tell in this polar darkness—to the muffled whine of a radio somewhere. Footsteps clanked down the hallway, and someone in a reflective vest peeked in. He spotted the group and said a few words in Danish, voice urgent.

The nurse intercepted him, then turned to Davis and Jillian. "He says the wind shifted. A big break might open in two or three hours. The helicopter from Nuuk can attempt a flight."

Ben scrubbed a hand across his face, blinking away the fog of half-sleep. Ingrid slept fitfully, but at least her breathing was stronger than before. The antibiotic might be working. She had a bit more color in her cheeks—still pale, but less ghostly.

Jillian roused as well, rubbing her stiff shoulders. "That's good news. We can get her out of here soon, maybe to a bigger hospital."

Ben's gaze slipped to the container on the floor. *And what about that?* he wondered. They'd have to decide soon. If they turned it over to some government contact, it might vanish into a black-ops lab. If they tried to destroy it outright, they might just be shifting the problem or risking a partial release. The moral quandary sat heavy in his gut.

Qannik rose from his chair by the door, stretching his neck until it cracked. He met Ben's eyes, quietly asking a question. Ben gave a small shake of his head— *We don't know yet.*

Dr. Davis looked up from where he'd just taken Ingrid's blood pressure. "Who's hungry?" He grimaced. "I saw a vending machine in the hall. Not exactly five-star, but we need energy."

Ben nodded. "I'll chip in whatever coins I've got."

As they rummaged for spare change, Jillian wandered over to him, gaze drifting to the container. "When Ingrid's stable and that helicopter shows," she murmured, "we're taking it with us, right?"

Ben nodded slowly. "Absolutely. I'm not letting this thing out of my sight until we're sure it's secure. We'll bring it on the chopper to a hospital or an air base—somewhere with real quarantine protocols." He paused. "I know we can't just keep it secret forever. But let's get Ingrid well first."

She gave a faint smile, though worry lines remained on her brow. "Agreed. One crisis at a time."

Ben stooped to check the container's latch once more, ensuring it was still sealed. Then, without a word, he followed her out to the corridor, where they rummaged through the vending machine for stale candy bars and lukewarm bottled water. It was a far cry from the feast they deserved, but it would do. They sat on a bench, unwrapping the bars, munching in companionable exhaustion.

Behind them, the wind rattled the windows. Occasionally, the lights flickered, but the generator held. Qannik paced the hallway, half on guard duty, half trying to walk off the tension. Dr. Davis dozed for a brief moment in a plastic chair. Ingrid slept in measured breaths.

No one spoke of the station's bodies lying under sheets in empty corridors, or of the mercenaries locked in a closet, or of Dr. Falk's dream project twisted into a nightmare. Not yet. That reckoning would come soon enough, once they had the strength to face it.

CHAPTER 13

BEN STOOD near the clinic's small front window, scanning the slate-gray sky for any sign of rotors. His breath fogged the glass. Behind him, Jillian paced in tight circles, arms wrapped around herself. Qannik had stationed himself by Ingrid's makeshift cot, looking like a protective statue. A half hour ago, they were certain a medevac helicopter was inbound to whisk Ingrid away to a better-equipped hospital. Now, the updates on the radio were sounding grim.

A burst of static crackled from the console on a nearby table. Dr. Davis moved closer to the speaker, fiddling with the dial as a Greenlandic dispatcher's voice came through in English. "*—low visibility... turbulence... no go. Apologies. The chopper can't fly in this weather, over.*"

Jillian stopped pacing. "Did they just say they're scrubbing the flight?"

Ben exhaled. "Sounds like it. They can't risk the approach. That means no medevac until the weather calms."

Dr. Davis pressed the talk button. "Understood. Thanks for trying. Over."

Static. Then silence.

It felt like a punch to the gut. Ingrid was stable for now, but how long would that last? They'd already lost enough time. Ben glanced at the black container near the wall—a silent reminder of how high the stakes really were.

Jillian raked a hand through her hair. "So we're stuck here waiting?"

Dr. Davis shook his head, frustration and worry etched across his features. "Her fever's lower, but she's still nowhere near healthy. We can't stay in this half-equipped clinic indefinitely. The local staff doesn't have the resources she needs. If her infection resurges, or if that virus is truly in her system..." He trailed off, lips pressed tight.

Qannik's voice was low but firm. "What about Mara? Could she fly us out? She's worked this region for a while, so she's no stranger to storms like this."

Ben shot a wary glance at the window, where Mara's plane sat under a coating of snow. They'd used it to get off the ice sheet in the first place, but he wasn't thrilled about continuing to trust a prop transport in these conditions. "She seems capable," he said, "but is it safe?"

Jillian shrugged. "No. But we're out of options."

A soft moan from Ingrid pulled them closer. She stirred, blinking weakly. Dr. Davis bent down, checking her pulse and the status of her IV. "Her vitals are okay at the moment, but a relapse could be fatal," he murmured. "We need a real hospital—somewhere with an ICU."

Ben frowned at the swirling clouds outside. "If the helicopter can't fly, maybe a small plane has a better shot, especially if it's outfitted with skis. Mara might do it."

Jillian raised her chin. "I'll go talk to Mara. She's probably going stir-crazy, too."

Ben sighed. "I'll come with. Qannik, keep an eye on Ingrid."

They trudged out of the clinic into a brisk wind. It wasn't the howling blizzard of the interior ice sheet, but it stung enough to make Ben squint. The air smelled of diesel from the airport's limited ground vehicles. They rounded a corner, spotting Mara working on her plane's engine cowling under a portable floodlight. She looked up at their approach.

"You two look grim," she said, wiping grease from her fingers.

Jillian cut right to the chase. "Helicopter's grounded. Ingrid's stuck here unless we find another route. We were hoping you'd fly us out."

Mara's gaze flicked from Jillian to Ben, then to the distant clinic. "I heard over the local chatter. Storm's hitting the chopper routes pretty hard." She zipped up her jacket, exhaling steam. "But taking my plane's no picnic, either. Those winds are savage above three thousand feet. Where do you want to go—Nuuk?"

Ben exchanged a look with Jillian. Nuuk, the capital, had the best-equipped hospital in Greenland. It was the logical choice, and from there they could figure out the rest—like calling in the CSO for the virus containment. "Yeah," he said. "Nuuk."

Mara drummed her fingertips on the plane's side, mulling it over. "I can try. No promises we won't hit nasty turbulence. Fuel's good, I've done some maintenance. We'll need to strip out any extra weight to make room for Ingrid's stretcher. You ready to go soon?"

Ben's relief warred with a lingering worry, but he nodded anyway. "We're ready as soon as you are."

She waved them off. "Give me twenty minutes to double-check everything, then bring your patient and your gear. We'll do a short hop to Nuuk—couple hours max, if the weather holds."

Jillian's face lit with gratitude. "Thank you."

Mara shrugged, avoiding eye contact. "Yeah, well, I'm not heartless. I saw what Ingrid went through." Her tone was odd, but not overtly hostile.

Ben frowned slightly. "We appreciate it," he said, meaning it. "Just let us know when you're ready."

They headed back to the clinic, where Dr. Davis and Qannik had already started prepping Ingrid for transport: bundling her in extra coats and blankets, setting up a portable IV bag that would hang from the plane's interior rigging. Ingrid murmured incoherently, obviously exhausted.

"Is Mara in?" Qannik asked, glancing up.

Ben nodded. "She'll try for a flight. We have to move soon. She's checking the plane."

CHAPTER 14

A WAVE of tension broke into the room—everyone had been on edge, waiting for the verdict. Dr. Davis exhaled relief, carefully adjusting Ingrid's oxygen flow. "All right, let's not waste time."

They gathered what few supplies the clinic could spare: a couple antibiotic vials, spare bandages, a small battery-powered heart monitor. Jillian made sure the black container of virus samples was sealed and locked. Ben hefted it, as familiar now as a well-worn backpack, though far more dangerous.

One of the local nurses helped them wheel Ingrid out on the stretcher, up a gentle ramp and across the icy tarmac. Mara was crouched by her plane's cargo hatch, rearranging gear to make space. She stood, motioning them forward. "Put her right here. I cleared a spot and strapped down a board as a makeshift bed."

They eased Ingrid in, careful not to jar her. Dr. Davis climbed in after her, hooking the IV to a metal bar on the plane's interior. Qannik followed, carrying spare medical gear. Ben slid in last, gingerly placing the container near his seat. Jillian squeezed in beside him, arms hugging her sides for warmth. The small plane felt claustrophobic.

Mara pulled the hatch shut, sealed it, then hopped into the cockpit. She donned a headset, flipping switches. The engine coughed to life in a roar, propellers spinning. Through a grimy window, Ben saw airport staff waving them forward. In no time, they were taxiing down the short runway, the plane sliding over uneven patches of ice.

Dr. Davis kneeled at Ingrid's side, one hand on her pulse. Jillian shared a tense look with Ben. The container's presence loomed like an unspoken threat between them. If they could just get to Nuuk safely, they'd have a real hospital, real labs, maybe a secure handoff for these vials. This was the last hurdle.

The plane's acceleration pinned them against their seats. Mara lifted off, skis skimming the ice until they gained altitude. For a few terrifying seconds, the wind buffeted them sideways, and Ben clenched his jaw. Then the aircraft steadied, climbing into the dull, overcast sky. Kangerlussuaq shrank below, its snow-swept runways vanishing behind a swirl of cloud.

Mara's voice crackled over the tiny overhead speaker. "We're in the air. Should be a smoother ride above these clouds, but hang on."

Jillian let out a breath, tension easing from her shoulders. Dr. Davis adjusted Ingrid's blanket. Qannik braced his legs, glancing warily at the windows.

They flew in relative silence for about twenty minutes, the drone of the engine punctuated by Ingrid's occasional whimper. Dr. Davis checked her vitals, nodding to himself. "Her temperature's still better than it was. We just have to keep her from shifting around too much."

Ben patted the container, more out of habit than anything. He shot Jillian a small, cautious smile. They might actually pull this off.

Another ten minutes passed. The plane soared above a thinning layer of cloud, revealing slivers of Greenland's jagged coast. Snow-capped mountains jutted like teeth. Ben wondered if they might see a break in the weather soon.

Mara's voice broke through the cabin speaker. "Folks, I need a quick word with your fearless leader back there. Ben, mind joining me up front?"

Ben glanced at Jillian, arching a brow. She looked just as surprised as he did. But maybe Mara needed navigational help or wanted to confirm their flight plan. He unbuckled, carefully stepping around Ingrid's stretcher. The plane jolted in a bit of turbulence, forcing him to grip a seat for balance.

He slid into the copilot's seat, snapping a spare headset over his ears. Mara's face was partially shadowed by the overhead instruments, but her eyes flicked to him with an unreadable expression.

"Everything okay?" he asked, adjusting the microphone at his mouth.

She nodded at the altimeter. "We're cruising at about eight thousand feet, nice and easy. The wind's calmer. We should make Nuuk in about two hours, maybe less if the forecast holds." She paused, lips twisting in a half-smile. "I wanted to ask you something."

Ben's gut prickled. "Sure."

"Why'd you bring that container? Seems risky. We could have left it behind, dealt with it later. Ingrid's the priority, right?"

He gave a cautious shrug. "We can't risk it falling into the wrong hands. Station's compromised, mercs are locked up there, but who knows what might happen. This virus is too dangerous to leave lying around."

She nodded slowly. "Right. Too dangerous."

Something in her tone set him on edge. Maybe his instincts were just rattled.

He shifted in his seat. "Mara... thanks again for doing this. We owe you."

She glanced at him, a slight curve to her mouth. "You do, don't you?"

A surge of turbulence rocked the plane before he could reply. Mara corrected smoothly, ignoring the bounce. Ben gripped the seat, heart jumping. That wasn't normal turbulence—it felt more like a sudden turn.

He squinted at the panel. The heading indicator showed a slight deviation from the route to Nuuk. "Hey, are we off course?"

Mara tapped the controls, leveling the plane. "Wind push, that's all," she said in a maddeningly calm voice. "Don't worry."

Ben eyed her. She kept her left hand on the yoke, the right near the throttle. Something about her posture was tense, coiled.

She cleared her throat. "You know, a virus that valuable... must be worth a fortune to the right buyer."

His blood went cold. *Here it is.* He tried to keep his voice even. "Don't start. You know we can't let that thing loose."

Mara gave a humorless chuckle, still staring straight ahead. "We can't, but we might. I've got a contact who'd pay enough to set us all up for life. I figure you're the practical type, Bennett. We could do this together."

He shook his head, feeling his pulse pound. "We're not selling it. Don't ask again."

CHAPTER 15

HER LEFT HAND stayed on the controls, but her right hand slid discreetly behind the pilot's seat. She withdrew a small pistol, resting it on her thigh, hidden from the cabin. Ben's stomach twisted.

She shot him a sidelong glance. "I had a feeling you'd say that. Shame."

He forced calm, glancing at the door behind him. If he shouted, Qannik or Jillian would come running—but in the cramped space, Mara could snap off a shot before they'd get there. Not to mention the plane was in the air, and she was the pilot.

"Mara," he said, keeping his voice low, "think carefully. If you do anything stupid, we all go down. Ingrid, Jillian, Dr. Davis—innocent people."

Her jaw set. "Innocent, sure. They wouldn't have to die if you'd just see sense. People pay millions for half-baked biotech. This virus? Triple that. And you think you'll lock it in a vault? You're kidding yourself."

He weighed his odds. She had the advantage, but he had to try. "We'll hand it off to the right authorities. No one else. That's final."

She let out a disdainful snort. "Fine. Guess I'll do it the hard way."

In one fluid motion, she thrust the yoke forward. The plane pitched violently downward, and Ben's stomach lurched. He scrabbled for a hold, crashing against the console. Mara jerked the pistol up, pointing it at him with one hand while she stabilized the dive with the other.

Behind them, a chorus of shouts rang out. Jillian and Qannik must have been thrown off balance. Ingrid's stretcher likely slid. Dr. Davis yelled something about watching the IV.

Ben braced himself, knuckles white on the seat. "Pull up!"

Mara's grin was icy. "I will. Once you promise to give me that container."

He swallowed a surge of panic. "You'll kill us both at this angle."

She eased back on the yoke an inch, just enough to slow the dizzying descent. "I'm a damn good pilot, Bennett. We're not going to crash, unless *I* decide to. Now, how about it? You give me the container, I drop you off in Nuuk, no one else has to get hurt."

His mind spun. If he gave it to her, everything they'd fought for was gone. The virus would be in the wind. But if he refused, she might throw them into a death spiral.

"I need your answer," she said, voice tight.

He glanced at her gun, then at the altimeter. They were still in a shallow dive. The needle ticked downward, thousands of feet slipping away. A few more seconds of this, and Qannik or Jillian might come barreling in—he had to stall.

"Mara," he said slowly, "the container's in the main cabin. You'd have to go back there to get it."

She shook her head, hair whipping across her forehead. "So call Jillian to bring it up. Use that cabin intercom."

He hesitated, breath ragged. Maybe if Jillian got close, she could see the gun and... do what? Tackle Mara? In these tight quarters, a single stray bullet might punch through the cockpit window or the fuselage.

She prodded him with the pistol barrel. "Now, or I pitch us steeper."

Ben switched on the intercom with a trembling finger. "Jillian... I need you up here. Bring the container."

Mara nodded, eyes scanning the horizon. She pulled back slightly on the yoke, leveling them out a bit. The plane's engine roared, wind beating against the windows.

Down the aisle, Jillian's voice was muffled but urgent. "Ben? Is everything all right?"

He forced calm into his tone. "Just... come up here with it. Hurry."

"Okay, hold on—" She sounded suspicious, but he prayed she wouldn't barge in recklessly.

They waited, the plane rattling. Mara kept the gun trained on him, her jaw tight. He had no illusions: the moment she had the container in her hands, all bets were off. He silently willed Jillian and Qannik to figure out a plan.

Footsteps. Jillian appeared in the narrow doorway behind them, the container tucked against her chest. One glance at Mara's pistol and the angle of the plane told her everything. Her eyes widened. "Mara, what are you doing?"

Mara flicked the muzzle toward Jillian, then back at Ben, indecisive about which threat was more pressing. "I'm taking what's owed," she said. "Hand it over, and I'll let you land with me."

Jillian's posture coiled. "You can't. This virus... you'll doom countless people."

A flash of fury crossed Mara's face. "Save the sermon. Slide it onto the copilot's seat, right in front of you, or I nosedive this plane."

Jillian licked her lips, knuckles white on the handle. Ben met her gaze, trying to send a silent message: *Stall.*

Jillian edged forward, glancing to see if Qannik was behind her. He wasn't visible, maybe dealing with Ingrid or waiting for a cue. She slowly crouched, setting the container on the seat. The plane hit another pocket of turbulence, jostling them all. Mara cursed, wresting the yoke, which momentarily pointed the pistol off-target. Ben tensed, ready to lunge—

But Mara whipped the gun back, reading his intent. "Don't try it," she snarled. "Both of you, back up. Let me get the container."

Jillian retreated a step, hands up. Ben forced himself to do the same. Mara pulled the plane's yoke level, letting out a ragged breath. Carefully, she reached over with her right hand, never taking her eyes off them. Her fingers closed around the container's handle.

"That's better," she said through gritted teeth. She lifted it onto her lap, eyes gleaming with triumph. "Now, we'll continue to Nuuk, but you breathe a word of this to anyone, I'll swear you forced me under threat. Understood?"

Ben's stomach churned. She had the advantage—the plane, the gun, the virus. He exchanged a desperate look with Jillian. Ingrid's life hung in the balance, not to mention their own.

"You're making a big mistake," Jillian hissed.

Mara ignored her, turning to the instrument panel. "Sit. Strap in. Don't try anything. I'll land us close enough to the hospital, then we part ways. If you're smart, you'll walk away with your lives."

CHAPTER 16

BEN STARED out the cockpit window, struggling to keep his breathing steady. Clouds swirled beyond the glass, blanketing the view in a cold haze. The plane's interior felt claustrophobic now that Mara had drawn her weapon. The small space magnified every sound: the whoosh of air through vents, the rhythmic thrum of the propellers, Jillian's too-quick breathing behind him.

Mara held the pistol casually, but he sensed her tension. She gripped the virus container with her free hand, keeping it on her lap like a treasured purse. Between them lay the narrow plane console—levers, dials, the single yoke that she clutched like a lifeline. If she jerked that stick too hard in either direction, they'd all spiral.

Jillian shifted on her feet, arms half-raised as if trying to show she meant no harm. "Mara," she said evenly, "we need to check on Ingrid. She's in the back with Dr. Davis and Qannik. She's still fragile."

Mara lifted a brow, eyes flicking to Jillian in the overhead mirror. "You can check on her. Just stay where I can see you. And don't try anything cute."

Jillian nodded stiffly, moving out of Ben's line of sight. He couldn't see her once she crossed behind the pilot's seat, but he heard the shuffle of her boots on the thin carpet.

He swallowed hard, forcing down the urge to lash out. If he grabbed Mara's wrist, maybe he could wrestle the gun away—but one wrong angle on the yoke, and they'd nosedive. And he had a feeling Mara knew how to push the plane, how to send them into a deadly spin if necessary.

A shudder rolled through the fuselage. Turbulence. Mara muttered a curse, adjusting their heading. "This storm's not letting up. I might have to descend if it gets too rough."

Ben tried to keep his voice calm. "Descend where?"

She shrugged. "Somewhere remote, safe enough to land. Then I'll sort out my next step. Maybe you all get to walk away, maybe not. Depends on you."

"Fine," he said. "Let's just... keep it steady until we're out of the worst clouds."

"Sure." She paused, glancing sideways. "But no sudden moves. I'd hate for Ingrid to pay the price if you get heroic."

He felt a spike of anger at that. Threatening Ingrid, who was barely clinging to health, was low—about as low as it got. But he forced himself to keep still. A confrontation right now was suicide.

From behind came the low murmur of voices. Jillian speaking softly, probably to Qannik and Dr. Davis. Maybe giving them a rundown. A minute later, Jillian reappeared in the aisle, standing carefully where Mara could see her.

"She's stable," Jillian said, "but not great. Davis says her fever might be creeping back up. We need to land soon—at an actual hospital."

Mara snorted. "We'll land where I say. We may not have a choice in this wind."

Jillian bristled, but Ben motioned for her to keep her cool. Another jolt of turbulence rattled the cockpit. Mara cursed, pulling back on the throttle. A glance at the altimeter showed they were descending slightly, perhaps a thousand feet lower.

Ben wondered if that might be a good thing. At lower altitude, the temperature might be warmer, meaning less risk of severe icing. Or maybe it was just trading one hazard for another: heavier winds at lower levels. Hard to say. Mara seemed to have experience in these conditions—she'd proven it before.

He cleared his throat. "Look, you got what you wanted: the container. You don't have to keep a gun on me. I'm not gonna crash the plane with Ingrid onboard."

She shot him a sideways glare. "Maybe not intentionally, but I know your type. You're too noble. Too righteous. You'd do something stupid if you thought it might save the day."

He swallowed. "Then think about Ingrid. She's innocent. Doesn't deserve to die for some black-market score."

Mara's jaw tightened. "Don't lecture me. I didn't say I wanted anyone dead. I just want the virus under my control."

Jillian, still halfway in the aisle, inhaled sharply. "What's your plan? Sell it to some shady biotech group? Let them tear it apart and re-engineer it?"

Mara's knuckles whitened on the yoke. "I have a buyer. That's all you need to know. And yeah, they'll pay big. Everyone's got a price, even you. If you'd listened, we could've split it."

Ben's heart thudded. "You think that's how this ends? You waltz in with a weaponized virus, collect a bag of money, and vanish?"

She said nothing, but her silence spoke volumes.

Jillian's voice quivered with anger. "You do realize it's not just money on the table. This virus could start a pandemic."

Mara blew out a sharp breath. "I doubt it. The buyer's not a terrorist—they're a pharma group. They want exclusive rights, maybe to develop a miracle cure. Or maybe sell the threat. Either way, that's not my problem."

"It will be when thousands die," Jillian snapped.

"Enough!" Mara barked. She turned the plane slightly, heading westward. "This conversation's over."

The cabin fell into tense silence, broken only by the engine's unrelenting drone. Ben's mind spun. *We have to do something.* If Mara truly intended to land somewhere remote—he guessed a hidden runway or patch of flat ice—she could offload the container, arrange a pickup, and vanish. Even if Ingrid survived the flight, the virus would be lost to the black market.

He shot Jillian a meaningful look. *Any ideas?* She stared back, eyes flicking to the corridor, maybe thinking about Qannik. If Qannik could sneak up behind Mara, catch her off guard, they might have a chance to disarm her. But she was hyper-vigilant, and the cockpit was cramped.

Another shudder rocked the plane. This one was worse, sending a coffee thermos clattering from Mara's seat pocket. She swore, leveling out the wings. "Stupid crosswinds. I might have to drop below the clouds completely if this keeps up."

Ben steadied himself on the console. "That might be good," he said, feigning helpfulness. "Less turbulence down low, right?"

She eyed him suspiciously. "Sometimes, but it depends on the terrain. Mountains can whip the wind into rotors. And visibility might be shot."

Jillian spoke up, carefully modulating her tone. "We're still heading for Nuuk, correct?"

Mara gave a hollow laugh. "Not exactly. I told you, we're going somewhere safe for me to meet my contact, then we'll continue to Nuuk."

Ben's gut clenched. "How far from here?"

Mara shrugged. "An hour. Maybe less. We'll see if the weather cooperates. Don't worry about it."

Jillian's hands balled at her sides. "You promised you'd at least let Ingrid get real medical help."

Mara's mouth thinned. "I said I'd see what I can do. No guarantees."

Ben's head pounded. *We can't just let her steer us off course.* Maybe there was a way to sabotage the plane's instruments or redirect them at the last second. But that was too risky—especially with Ingrid in such fragile shape. If they crashed, everything was lost.

CHAPTER 17

THE PLANE RUMBLED through another patch of rough air. This time, Ben heard a metallic whine behind them, as if something in the cargo area had shifted. Mara flicked a glance over her shoulder, obviously unsettled by the noise. In that second, her pistol wavered slightly, muzzle dipping. Ben tensed, but again, he didn't have a clear angle. She snapped her gaze back on him, gun snapping back up.

No luck there.

Jillian forced a calm question. "Do you at least have gear to keep Ingrid's stretcher secure if we land on rough ice?"

Mara smirked. "I did a quick rig job, sure. I've landed on glaciers before. No big deal. Just pray Ingrid doesn't need resuscitation mid-landing."

Ben gritted his teeth. "Why risk her life at all? She's a scientist—she could help you negotiate. She'd know how to handle the virus. Work with her, not against her."

The pilot's laugh was short, humorless. "I'm not some supervillain, Bennett. I just know when opportunity knocks. Now shut up and let me fly."

Ben and Jillian exchanged looks. Then Jillian backed away a step, returning to the cabin. Maybe she wanted to regroup with Qannik and Dr. Davis, or check on Ingrid. Ben stayed put, pinned by Mara's gaze.

His thoughts churned. *If we do nothing, we land in God-knows-where, and Mara sells the virus. If we act now, she might pitch us into a fatal dive.* The tension was almost unbearable.

Minutes dragged by in suffocating silence. At some point, the altimeter ticked lower again, the plane descending through thinner cloud. Sunlight threatened to pierce the gloom, giving glimpses of jagged peaks far below. Mara breathed evenly, adjusting knobs, occasionally barking at Ben to keep his hands visible on the console.

Then, from behind, a muffled clang and a shout. Mara stiffened, half-turning her head. "What was that?"

Ben took his chance. He lunged, grabbing for her wrist. She yelped, the plane bucking as she jerked the yoke. The pistol fired once, deafeningly loud in the cockpit. Ben flinched, feeling heat graze his shoulder. A bullet smashed through the windshield's corner, spiderwebbing the glass. Wind screamed in through the crack, buffeting them with frigid air. Mara snarled, fighting him off with surprising strength.

Jillian lunged back into view, but the cramped cockpit left no room to help. The plane tilted wildly. Ben wrestled with Mara's arm, struggling to keep the muzzle away from both of them, while her other hand clutched the yoke, trying to regain control.

"Let go!" she screamed, eyes wild. She smashed the container into the side of Ben's head, sending stars across his vision. He lost his grip, reeling. Mara yanked back on the yoke, flattening the plane's dive. More shards of glass rattled from the bullet hole, the wind roaring.

She whipped the pistol around, but Jillian kicked at Mara's arm from behind, forcing her to shoot wide. The second shot shattered a side window, howling air ripping through the cabin. Ben ducked, feeling glass bite his cheek. The entire plane lurched dangerously to the left, altitude dropping.

Jillian tried to grab the container, but Mara twisted away, shrieking. She smashed the handle of the gun into Jillian's forehead. Jillian crashed against the cabin wall, dazed.

Ben shook off the dizzy haze. The pistol was still in Mara's hand, but her grip was loose. If he could just angle it away... Another jolt of turbulence slammed them. Mara fought with the controls, face contorted. She had to either hold the yoke or keep the gun on them—she couldn't do both well.

Somewhere behind them, Qannik yelled something, likely pinned down with Ingrid's stretcher or bracing Dr. Davis. The plane's engine whined at a dangerous pitch. The altimeter needle spun, losing altitude.

Mara grimaced. "Enough! You want us all dead?"

Ben lunged again. This time, he seized her pistol wrist with both hands, slamming it against the console. Her finger squeezed the trigger, loosing another wild shot that ricocheted behind them. Sparks showered. Then, with a grunt, he wrenched the gun free. It clattered to the floor near the rudder pedals.

Mara roared in fury, elbowing him in the ribs. He gasped, but kept pushing her hand away from the yoke. The plane dove hard, sending Jillian sprawling into the cockpit. They could hear the engine straining, the wind screaming through the shattered windows.

Jillian had blood on her forehead, but she latched onto the yoke as well.

Together, she and Mara wrestled for control. "We're gonna crash!" Jillian yelled, voice hoarse with adrenaline.

Ben groped for the gun on the floor—he couldn't see it, only hear it sliding underfoot. The plane nose pitched up and down, like a bucking horse. At this rate, they'd slam into the mountains below. Through the cracked windshield, he glimpsed the ground rushing closer—a patchwork of snow, rock, and steep ridges.

He finally located the pistol, pinning it with his knee. Mara realized too late, trying to kick him. "No!" she screamed. But Jillian jerked the yoke, forcing Mara off-balance.

Ben seized the weapon. He tried to lift it, only to find Mara's hand grabbing for the container again. She wouldn't let it go, even if it meant they all died. In that split-second decision, Ben jammed the gun's muzzle at the plane's floor and pulled the trigger, blowing a hole straight through the metal. Wind roared through the new gap.

Mara flinched, stumbling just enough for Jillian to yank the container free. Mara clawed at it, but Jillian twisted around, pressing her weight against the seat. The plane pitched violently to the right.

Ben braced himself, chest heaving. They were in a near free fall now, altitude dangerously low. He looked up, saw the ridges looming. "Pull up! Pull up!" he shouted.

Jillian threw her shoulder into Mara, knocking her aside. Then she yanked back on the yoke with both hands. The engine coughed in protest as the nose rose, hugging the slope of a mountainside.

An ear-splitting scrape—something clipped the underbelly. The impact jolted them so hard that Ben's teeth rattled. The plane bounced off the slope, spinning in mid-air for a terrifying instant before Jillian corrected enough to skim past a rocky outcrop.

Then, just as it seemed they might climb away, the engine sputtered. Another lurch. They slammed down onto a snowy plateau, skidding in a shower of ice and debris. Metal screamed. The plane tore across the ground, half airborne, half crashing. Ben's vision blurred. He heard Qannik yelling Ingrid's name. Dr. Davis shouting in terror.

Finally, the plane lurched to a stop with a grinding shriek. The left wing crumpled against a jagged rock. Wind whipped through every bullet hole and broken window. A hush fell, punctuated only by the rattling of the battered propeller spinning to a dead stop.

Ben tasted blood. His ears rang. Smoke drifted from the cockpit console. The plane was half-buried in snow, angled precariously. He coughed, turning to see Jillian slumped against the pilot's seat, eyes fluttering, the container clutched to her chest.

And then he blacked out.

CHAPTER 18

BEN FORCED HIS EYES OPEN, fighting the dull throb at the back of his skull. For a fleeting, blissful moment, he forgot where he was. Then reality hit him: the crashed plane, the howling wind, the sting of frigid air seeping through the torn fuselage.

He turned his head. The left side of the cockpit was crushed into a ragged, twisted shape. At some point, he must have blacked out—his memory ended with Jillian wrestling the controls and a bone-jarring collision. Now, the plane's engines were silent, the propellers half-buried in a drift. The only sounds were the creak of warped metal and the distant moan of wind.

Behind him, Qannik and Dr. Davis were already scrambling, checking Ingrid's stretcher, shouting for assistance.

Ben's head pounded. They'd survived the crash—but at what cost? He forced a shallow breath, gaze sliding to Jillian and the container. *At least the virus didn't vanish into Mara's hands,* he told himself.

Outside, through the shattered windshield, he saw a desolate expanse of ice and rock.

No sign of civilization. No sign of rescue.

They were stranded in the middle of nowhere, wounded, with an unstable patient and a compromised aircraft. But they were alive.

Slowly, he tested each limb for injury. A few cuts, a bruised rib, but he could move. He found his seatbelt still fastened. With numb fingers, he popped the buckle. The cabin spun for a second. He braced himself, gulping back nausea.

Jillian.

He shoved aside a chunk of paneling and spotted her slumped against the pilot's seat, eyes shut. Blood matted her hair, and her breathing was ragged. Panic flared in him. He scrambled closer. "Jillian?" he croaked, voice cracking. She stirred, letting out a soft moan. At least she was alive.

"Ben...?" Her eyelids fluttered, unfocused. A gash on her forehead had bled heavily, staining one side of her face a ghastly crimson.

"It's me," he said, gently wiping away some of the drying blood with his coat sleeve. "Take it easy. You're hurt."

She swallowed hard, trying to focus. "Engine died... we clipped... rock..."

"Yeah. We crashed. Are you in pain?"

She let out a shaky laugh that turned into a grimace. "Everything hurts. My leg is... God, I can't move it well."

Ben nodded, scanning her left leg twisted awkwardly under the seat. He winced. "Don't try yet. We'll get help. Let me check the others."

He crawled over the toppled cockpit console, shards of glass crunching under his boots. The side window was shattered, letting in a constant swirl of snow. "Qannik? Dr. Davis?" he called, voice echoing.

A muffled shout came from the back. "Here!" It was Qannik. "Ingrid's bad off. Davis is working on her."

Ben found them near the cargo space, Ingrid still strapped to her makeshift stretcher. Qannik braced her shoulders while Dr. Davis hovered, checking her vitals. The plane's interior was canted at an angle, and Ingrid's face looked ashen, her breathing shallow. Davis's coat was smeared with blood. Possibly Ingrid's. Possibly Jillian's. Possibly all of theirs.

"How is she?" Ben asked, crawling closer.

Davis shook his head grimly. "Her fever's spiked again. Impact must've jolted her pretty hard. She's still unconscious—barely stable."

Ben's chest tightened. Ingrid had been near death even before the crash. Now, they were stranded on some godforsaken slope in the middle of Greenland's wilderness, no help in sight. If her infection—or that ancient virus—continued to ravage her...

He took a breath to steady himself. "We'll figure it out. Let me see if the radio works."

Qannik scowled, scanning the torn hull. "Wind's blowing straight through those holes. Temperature's dropping."

Ben noticed, too—his breath already fogged in front of him. The plane wouldn't keep them warm for long, and even if there was some battery power left, the heater was probably destroyed in the crash. They needed shelter, or rescue, or both.

He pulled himself toward the radio panel near the tail section. Wires hung in tangled loops, sparks occasionally flickering where something shorted. He flicked a few switches, but the LED readouts stayed dark. Another flick, a static pop—and then nothing.

He slammed a fist on the ruined panel. "Dead."

Dr. Davis clenched his jaw. "We need to keep Ingrid from crashing, medically speaking. I'm running low on IV fluid, and she's losing ground."

Ben glanced around for the black container—the virus. Fear jabbed him anew. *If that thing's cracked open...* But no, by sheer luck it lay wedged under a collapsed seat, intact. Some cosmic irony: the virus was still safe while the rest of them fell apart.

He crawled back to Jillian. "Stay awake," he pleaded, tapping her cheek lightly. "We need you."

She let out a tight hiss of pain, nodding. "Won't pass out," she mumbled, though her face had gone pale. "Just... do something about the cold."

Ben had no illusions: with the plane's body twisted open, they'd freeze to death by nightfall, especially Ingrid. He wondered if the plane's emergency kit had survived—maybe a flare gun, some thermal blankets.

Qannik rummaged through overhead compartments, tossing out a battered first-aid kit, a few small blankets, and one orange flare. He cursed under his breath. "We're better off building a snow cave than expecting this to keep us alive."

Ben forced out a humorless chuckle. "Let's not drag Ingrid out into the snow if we can help it."

They settled into a grim routine for the next few hours, or what felt like hours—time blurred in the endless daylight that never quite looked like day. Dr. Davis did what he could for Ingrid, changing her IV bag. Qannik helped splint Jillian's leg, improvising with a metal rod from the plane's interior. Jillian fought through the agony in silence.

Ben tried to block the jagged openings with scraps of seat cushions, stray luggage, anything to shield them from the worst of the wind. It worked, sort of. By the end, the plane looked like a patchwork nest, air whistling through cracks.

At some point, a hush descended. The wind calmed slightly. Snow drifted lazily against the plane's fuselage. Ingrid's shallow breathing rattled in the quiet. Ben knelt by her, pressing a hand to her fevered forehead. She was dangerously close to slipping away. He muttered a low curse, feeling helpless.

Then Qannik's head snapped up, ears pricked. "You hear that?"

Ben froze, listening. A faint whine, growing louder, maybe an engine. But not an airplane—more like snowmobiles. Could it be a rescue team?

He exchanged a cautious look with Qannik. "Let's not assume they're friendly," he murmured.

CHAPTER 19

THEY BOTH GRABBED the plane's battered rifles—one from the sub-level scuffle with the mercs, one from Mara's stash—and positioned themselves near the side hatch. Dr. Davis crouched protectively by Ingrid's stretcher and Jillian's huddled form. Her eyes were open, but she looked barely conscious.

The noise grew, distinct now: multiple engines. Through a gap in the torn fuselage, Ben glimpsed dark shapes zipping across the snow, leaving long trails behind them. Five, maybe six snowmobiles. He squinted. "Big group."

Qannik's brow furrowed. "Likely not random explorers. Looks like they know right where we are."

Ben's pulse thudded. He thought of Mara. She'd tried to sell the virus. Could these be her buyers, come to collect?

The engines revved closer, circling around the crash site. One by one, the snowmobiles idled to a stop outside the plane's nose. Figures dismounted. Men in heavy coats, goggles, and tactical gear. All armed with rifles or sidearms.

Ben cursed under his breath. "Armed. Definitely not rescue."

One figure stepped forward, flipping up a tinted visor. He scanned the wreckage. Then he shouted, voice muffled by the wind, "We know you're alive in there! Come out slowly and no one gets hurt."

Ben felt his jaw clench. "Stay low," he whispered to Qannik. "We can't let them waltz off with the container."

His mind raced. There were at least half a dozen men, maybe more. They had the advantage of open ground and mobility. He had a crippled plane, two injured companions, a near-dead Ingrid, and a bullet-riddled environment for cover. Not great odds.

The man outside shouted again, "Pilot's name is Mara, right? She was supposed to deliver something to us. If she's alive, bring her out. We want that cargo."

Ben's heart hammered. He peeked through a crack. Mara lay near the cockpit, unconscious, a nasty bruise on her temple. It didn't look like she was waking up soon, if ever.

He turned to Qannik, voice low. "We can't just surrender. They'll take the virus, maybe kill us all."

Qannik's gaze was grim. "Agreed. We need a plan."

Ben's eyes roamed the small cabin. "We might be able to lure a few inside, take them out one at a time. But they'll realize if their friends don't come back. Then we're pinned."

Jillian let out a shaky breath, straining to speak. "If they want the container, maybe... lead them away from Ingrid." Her words were forced, each breath costing her.

Dr. Davis shook his head fiercely. "You can't move."

She gestured feebly. "Ben can. Bait them... out there. Then Qannik picks them off."

Ben considered it—risky. But if these buyers thought the container might be stashed outside, they might chase him. "Could work," he muttered. "But six on one is still tough."

Qannik's lips thinned. "I can watch from a window, maybe snipe a few before they react. But you'll need to draw them far enough so they won't shoot the plane."

Ben patted the battered rifle. "How many shots do we even have?"

Qannik checked. "Six in this one. Mara's stash had a partial mag left, maybe eight rounds. Enough for a fight, if we're smart."

Outside, the lead man barked a final warning. "We're coming in if you don't respond. Last chance! Give us the cargo, and we might let you walk away."

Ben exhaled, adrenaline spiking. He had to decide immediately. "All right," he whispered. "I'll go out, act like I'm surrendering. Try to drag them away from the plane. Qannik, keep watch near the hatch. The moment you have a clear line, take it."

Qannik nodded, eyes like stone. "Don't get yourself killed."

"Working on it," Ben muttered, heart thudding.

Dr. Davis stayed crouched by Ingrid, jaw tight. "Be careful."

Jillian tried to offer him a reassuring look, but the pain twisted her features. "We're counting on you."

Ben swallowed, then crawled to the plane's side hatch. He pried it open just enough to slip through. The sudden blast of cold took his breath away. Gray daylight blanketed a broad, snow-blank plateau ringed by low ridges. The men stood in a semicircle near the nose. Their snowmobiles hummed quietly, exhaust trailing in the frozen air.

CHAPTER 20

HANDS RAISED, Ben stumbled forward, adopting a limp he didn't really have, just to look more beaten down. His breath plumed in front of him. "Don't shoot," he called, letting desperation creep into his voice. "We've got injured inside!"

The lead man, tall with a thick black beard, raised a gloved hand, signaling the others to hold fire. "Where's Mara?"

Ben jerked a thumb over his shoulder. "Unconscious. The crash. Some of us are alive, but... I can't move them easily." He plastered on a grimace. "We need help."

Black-Beard's eyes narrowed. "We're not exactly medics. Where's the cargo?"

Ben forced a hollow laugh, motioning vaguely to the plane. "Mara had it in the cockpit, I think. The plane's half-smashed." He let a nervous tremor creep into his voice. "You gotta help me find it."

A second man with a face mask barked, "Don't listen to this clown. He's stalling. We should go in, sweep the wreck. Take what we need."

Ben raised his hands higher. "Fine, sweep it. I'm just asking you not to kill our wounded. They won't fight. You can have whatever you want."

A sly look flickered in Black-Beard's eyes. "We came for the virus. That's it. Where exactly did Mara stash it?"

Ben gulped. "Well... the container got knocked around. I tried to move it, but it slipped under the plane's belly. I can show you."

He pointed behind them, toward the tail area, away from the hatch. The men exchanged glances. The one with the mask looked skeptical. "Under the plane? Why'd you drag it out there?"

Ben shrugged helplessly. "The fuselage was ripping apart. I thought I could shift it under the floor to keep it from falling off a cliff or something." He gestured again. "Come on, I'll show you. If you help me get it, it's yours. That's what you want, right?"

Black-Beard sniffed, then gestured for two men to follow. He signaled the others to flank out, rifles at the ready. Ben's pulse hammered as three men peeled off behind him, stepping into the plane's shadow, while the rest hung back near the nose. *Not quite what I hoped.* He'd wanted them all away, not half. But it might be enough.

He led them toward the plane's tail, which was partially buried in a mound of snow from the crash. The entire underside was crumpled. "It's wedged somewhere in there," he lied, playing up the timid act. He crouched, pretending to peer under the plane.

Black-Beard stepped in closer, aiming his rifle. "Move aside."

Ben took a shaky step back. "Sure, sure."

One of the other men knelt, pulling out a flashlight. The beam cut across the twisted metal. "Don't see anything."

Ben let out a theatrical sigh. "Maybe it slid further..."

Just then, the crash site erupted in gunfire. Qannik fired from the plane's side hatch, the bullet tearing into one of the men who'd stayed by the nose. He dropped instantly, rifle clattering. Another shot rang out—Qannik's second round clipped a second man's shoulder, spinning him to the ground with a scream.

All heads whipped toward the plane's fuselage. Black-Beard snarled, "Ambush!" He and his two men spun their rifles around, pointing away from Ben. *Perfect.*

Ben lunged. He grabbed Black-Beard's rifle barrel, yanking it down. The weapon roared, spitting a bullet into the snow at Ben's feet. The recoil jolted his arms, but adrenaline spiked. He slammed an elbow into Black-Beard's face, feeling the crunch of cartilage. The man stumbled back, cursing.

Another man swung at Ben with the butt of his rifle. Ben barely ducked in time, the metal grazing his ear. He drove a stiff jab into the attacker's gut, sending him staggering. Meanwhile, the third man aimed at Qannik's muzzle flash, opening fire. Bullets pinged off the plane's battered hull. Qannik returned fire, each shot echoing across the plateau.

The men near the nose scattered for cover behind snowmobiles. One tried to rev the engine, maybe to circle around. Qannik took a potshot, forcing them to hunker down.

Ben wrestled Black-Beard's rifle again, this time tearing it from his grip. The bearded man roared, swinging a wild punch. Ben blocked, pivoted, and used the rifle's stock like a club, striking Black-Beard's chest. He toppled, air whooshing from his lungs in a pained grunt.

The other two were on him instantly. One tackled Ben from behind, driving him face-first into the snow. The rifle flew from his grip. He tasted blood in his mouth. The second man kicked him in the side. Agony flared.

From the corner of his eye, he saw Qannik shoot another target near the plane's door. That man spun sideways, dropping behind a snowbank. The exchange was brutal, muzzle flashes strobing in the gloom.

Ben twisted, ignoring the pain in his ribs. He drove an elbow into the man's midsection, then jerked free. Rolling in the snow, he grabbed a fistful of powder and flung it into the attacker's face. The man sputtered, half-blind. Ben scrambled for the dropped rifle, fingers fumbling on the icy metal.

A bullet whizzed overhead—Black-Beard had drawn a sidearm. Ben ducked behind the plane's tail, heart pounding. Another bullet pinged off the fuselage, sending sparks. He had to neutralize these guys before they rallied.

The second man, still coughing snow from his mouth, charged. Ben rose onto a knee, bracing the rifle. He squeezed the trigger. The shot ripped through the man's shoulder, spinning him to the ground. A second shot, and the man stopped moving.

Black-Beard fired wildly. One round tore a gash in Ben's coat sleeve, skimming his arm. He hissed in pain, returning fire. The bullet caught Black-Beard in the thigh. The big man collapsed with a howl, dropping his pistol.

Ben staggered upright, scanning the chaos. Qannik had forced two others to retreat behind a snowmobile, but they fired potshots at the plane's hatch, pinning him down. Another lay motionless near the nose, blood staining the snow.

Ben gritted his teeth, stepping forward. "Drop it!" he bellowed, leveling the rifle at the two men behind the snowmobile. The battered plane, half-buried, offered Qannik partial cover, but these guys had line of sight on the hatch. If Qannik moved, they might tag him.

One of them popped up to shoot at Ben. He fired first. The bullet crashed through the man's chest. He pitched back, eyes wide. The last man cursed, dropping his rifle in surrender.

That left a handful of groaning bodies scattered across the crash site. Ben's lungs heaved, adrenaline surging. He scanned for any stragglers. Black-Beard lay gripping his thigh, blood seeping between his fingers. The pinned man near the snowmobile raised shaking hands, eyes darting fearfully.

It took a moment for the gunshots to stop echoing. Then Qannik emerged from the hatch, rifle still up, scanning. "Clear?" he shouted.

Ben exhaled. "Clear."

CHAPTER 21

HE KICKED away the leftover firearms and trudged back to Black-Beard, pressing a boot to the man's side to keep him from reaching that pistol again. "You trying to steal that virus?" he growled. "How's that working out for you?"

Black-Beard gritted his teeth, sweat beading on his forehead despite the cold. "We weren't... stealing. We had a deal with Mara. That's ours."

Ben snorted. "Not anymore. Where's your backup?"

A sarcastic chuckle, but the man didn't respond.

Ben pressed harder, making Black-Beard hiss in pain. "You better hope we find a rescue chopper before you bleed out."

He nodded to Qannik, who walked over and tossed the man's sidearm out of reach. The captive near the snowmobile stayed put, arms raised, cowering. The rest were either dead or incapacitated.

Qannik grimaced at the bodies. "We need to check on Ingrid and Jillian."

Ben's stomach churned, worry flooding back. He slung the rifle over his shoulder and limped toward the plane. Inside, Dr. Davis had propped Jillian against a chunk of seat. She breathed shallowly, eyes half-closed, her splinted leg trembling. Ingrid lay on her stretcher, no sign of improvement—just the shallow rise and fall of her chest.

Dr. Davis looked up at Ben. "Shots came close to us. Ingrid's still hanging on, but time's running out."

Ben raked a hand through his disheveled hair, the sting of the bullet graze smarting. "We cleared them—for now. Maybe they have supplies or a way to call out."

Qannik ducked back outside, rummaging the snowmobiles. He shouted from the other side of the wreck, "They've got sat-phones! And some gear."

A wave of relief hit Ben. With a working sat-phone, they might actually be able to call for help. He navigated the carnage carefully. Black-Beard lay on his back, cursing softly. The man who'd surrendered huddled behind a snowmobile, hands still raised. Qannik was rifling through a pack strapped on the seat, pulling out a satellite phone and a small metal case.

Ben joined him. "Good job. Let's see if that phone is functional."

Qannik flipped it open. A few bars of signal flickered. He pressed a button, waited. Static, then a faint dial tone. "We might have a chance here." He eyed the case. "Could be medical supplies?"

They pried it open. Inside were syringes, vials, something that looked suspiciously like sedation drugs. Not quite what they needed, but maybe it could stabilize Ingrid. Dr. Davis hurried over, rummaging through the kit with professional efficiency.

"That's a basic field kit, mostly opiates and broad-spectrum antibiotics," Davis muttered. "Could help Ingrid if she's in septic shock. Not perfect, but better than nothing."

Ben's shoulders sagged in relief. "Then do it. Save her."

Qannik kept scanning the other snowmobiles. "They have tents, fuel, more gear. Enough to ride out here for a while if need be. But let's call for extraction ASAP."

Ben nodded, stepping a few paces away to raise the sat-phone to his ear. The cold bit at his fingers, but he forced them steady. The phone dialed out, and after a few rings, a curt voice in Danish answered. *"Hallo?"*

He scrambled to recall the nearest authority or rescue unit. "Uh, English? Emergency. Plane crash near—" He paused, realizing he didn't know the exact coordinates.

Qannik overheard, grabbed the phone. "I can give them approximate GPS from the snowmobile's readout."

They huddled around the snowmobile's small screen, reading the blinking coordinates. Qannik relayed it in halting Danish. The voice on the other end grew sharp, rattling off questions. Qannik responded in calm, concise bursts. Finally, he ended the call and exhaled. "They'll send a rescue team if the weather window holds. Could be hours. Maybe half a day."

Ben glanced at Ingrid's stretcher. *Does she have half a day?*

He turned to Dr. Davis, who was already administering an antibiotic injection from the third-party kit. Jillian winced, holding her side. She tried to put on a brave face. "We'll... be okay," she murmured, though her pale complexion said otherwise.

Mara, unbelievably, still lay unconscious in the cockpit. Dr. Davis had thrown a tarp over her. If she woke, she'd find her buyers shot or captured. *Serves her right*, Ben thought grimly.

He knelt near the battered container, which Qannik must have set aside. The vials inside remained intact—a bizarre testament to how resilient — and dangerous — they were. He snapped it shut, relief flooding him that no stray bullets had cracked them.

Outside, the man who'd surrendered hovered anxiously, shooting glances at his wounded boss. Qannik secured them with leftover cable from the plane. They'd stay put until rescue arrived—assuming they didn't freeze.

Ben looked up at the sky. The clouds swirled, but he could see faint breaks of sun. That was something. He let out a long breath, the tension draining from his body, replaced by a bone-deep exhaustion. Ingrid needed real help soon, but for the moment, they had a lifeline: a sat-phone call to local authorities, enough supplies to keep her alive, and enough guns to discourage any further intrusion.

He trudged back to Jillian, squatting so their eyes were level. She looked at him, a shadow of a smile tugging at her cracked lips. "You did it?" she rasped.

He nodded, brushing a loose strand of hair from her face. "We did it. They're either dead or tied up. Qannik found a sat-phone—rescue's on its way."

Her eyes glistened with relief. "Tell Ingrid when she's awake."

He squeezed her hand. "You hang on, too, all right? Dr. Davis can handle your injuries until we get you to a hospital."

She closed her eyes, swallowing. "I'll hang on. Don't worry."

Ben scooted over to Ingrid's stretcher. Dr. Davis had set up a drip from the new antibiotic vials. She still looked pale, but a bit less on the brink. He gently took her hand. It was cold as ice. She didn't stir, but her chest rose and fell in shallow, steady breaths.

That was enough for now.

With the third-party mercenaries disarmed and a rescue team en route, they might actually survive this— and so might the world, protected from the horrors locked in that black container.

CHAPTER 22

BEN CROUCHED behind a jagged slab of twisted metal that had once formed part of the plane's fuselage. Snow whirled around him, catching the faint orange glow of the small fire Qannik had built near the starboard wing.

The hours since the crash had blurred together in a hazy slog of cold, pain, and desperate improvisation. He was spent—bone-weary, bruised, and bleeding. Yet he stayed alert, scanning the gloom for any further signs of trouble. After the last group of mercenaries had shown up to claim the virus, he wasn't about to take any more chances.

Behind him, the battered aircraft lay tilted at a precarious angle. Its left wing was crumpled against a rocky outcrop, and the cockpit windows were shattered from gunfire and impact. He could still see the faint glimmer of ice crystals on the exposed metal whenever the firelight danced across it.

Inside the plane, Ingrid hovered between life and death, her fever raging despite Dr. Davis's best efforts. Jillian lay semiconscious, her leg in a makeshift splint, drifting in and out of a restless doze.

The two mercenaries who were still alive remained bound and glowering, huddled against the cold.

And Mara, the treacherous pilot, was still unconscious in the cockpit, her fate uncertain.

Qannik had stoked the fire to a respectable blaze, feeding it chunks of seat foam, broken crates, and shards of splintered cabin walls. The rising flames offered a sliver of warmth, as well as a beacon for any rescue team braving the elements. Ben knew that the small victory of having a fire also meant they were, in some sense, advertising their location to anyone else who might come sniffing around.

But after fending off that last group of armed buyers, the adrenaline in his bloodstream was still thrumming, and he figured there was no point in hiding. They had already called for rescue—he just prayed it would be the right people showing up next time, not a second wave of mercenaries.

He tugged the collar of his jacket close, wincing as the movement pulled at a bruised shoulder. Every muscle in his body ached. On the ground beside him sat the black container: the virus. He had checked it for damage at least five times, each inspection revealing the same battered exterior but perfectly intact seals. That ironically robust design had allowed it to survive bullets, a plane crash, and now sub-zero temperatures.

He exhaled a visible plume of breath, half-resentful of how easily the container "endured" compared to the flesh-and-blood people who'd nearly died for it.

Dr. Davis appeared from behind a panel of bent fuselage, crawling on hands and knees. His face was tense, fatigue carving lines around his mouth. "Ingrid's temperature is sky-high again," he said in a hushed voice, as if the very air might carry off his words. "But she's holding on. I gave her another dose of the antibiotic we found in the mercenaries' pack. If we're lucky, it'll help slow any infection. She's too weak to fight off much of anything right now."

Ben nodded, forcing a grim smile. "She's stubborn." Ingrid had proven that more than once. "What about Jillian?"

A flicker of worry crossed Davis's eyes. "She's stable for the moment, but if we don't get that leg properly set soon, we risk permanent damage or worse. She's drifting in and out. I can only do so much here."

Ben glanced at the flickering shadows beyond the fire. "Have you heard anything back from the rescue team?"

Davis shook his head. "Radio's dead. We're down to the sat phone you lifted from the mercs, but I gave the rescue crew the number. I heard Qannik mention the battery was still good, but we have no incoming calls, no pings yet. We're just waiting."

The two men exchanged a look that carried exhaustion and a shard of hope. They'd done everything possible to keep people alive in a place that seemed hell-bent on taking lives. The cold pressed in from all sides, gnawing at their edges like some arctic predator.

If rescue didn't come soon, they'd be in a dire state. Ingrid had hours left, maybe a day at best. Jillian might be able to last longer, but pain and infection would set in. Even Qannik and Dr. Davis themselves were battered, walking around with bruised ribs, raw throats, throbbing headaches. Ben rubbed the cut near his own temple, grateful it had stopped bleeding for the most part.

A gust of wind spat smoke in his face. He turned away, eyes watering. "Let's keep the fire going," he rasped. "I'll take first watch. You try to get some rest."

Davis clapped him on the shoulder—gently, but it still hurt. "Don't hesitate to wake me if anything changes. I'll be inside with Jillian and Ingrid."

Ben watched the doctor disappear back into the gloom of the wrecked fuselage. For a moment, only the wind and the crackling flames kept him company. The mercenaries, all too aware of Qannik's watchful stance, kept quiet at the far edge of the plane's tail, bound together and shivering. One or two of them muttered curses in Ben's direction now and then, but none dared anything more risky. They probably knew their only chance of survival was to wait for rescue, the same as everyone else.

He crouched by the container, still torn about the deadly relic inside. The virus was the reason Dr. Falk and so many others had died, the reason Ingrid had nearly lost her life. He resented it, but he'd promised Ingrid—promised the entire team—that it wouldn't fall into the wrong hands. And that was exactly what he intended to ensure, even if it meant freezing here a bit longer.

Time passed in a weary haze. He adjusted the wood around the fire, stood up, paced, then sat again. At one point, Qannik came over with a scrap of tarp to block some of the wind, creating a tiny pocket of relative calm around the flames. Ben nodded thanks, mind churning with half-formed worries. The hours ticked by, the sky a swirling dome of cloud and haze.

Finally, just as the cold bit so deep that his teeth started chattering, the sat phone chirped to life. A faint ring, tinny and abrupt. Ben jolted. Qannik, who'd been dozing with his rifle across his lap, snapped awake. They exchanged a quick glance. Then Ben dug out the phone from his jacket, fumbling with numb fingers.

He pressed the green button. "Hello?" His voice sounded rough, foreign to his own ears.

Static hissed, then a man's voice emerged, distant but clear enough to understand. *"Mr. Bennett?"*

Ben's pulse spiked. He recognized the accent as American, though not one he'd heard from the previous unknown contacts or from the local rescue ops. "Yeah. Who's this?"

CHAPTER 23

"NAME'S GIVENS," the man answered. His tone was clipped, businesslike, but with a hint of unease. *"I'm with the group that was alerted to your position, and I work with Chambers, who you've already spoken with. We got your coordinates passed to us from local authorities in Greenland. My team is inbound, but we've had trouble with the weather. Mind telling me your status?"*

Ben swallowed, almost laughing at how complicated that question was. "Plane's crashed, we've got wounded, a couple of mercs tied up, and we're about half-frozen. Aside from that, all sunshine and rainbows."

Givens let out a small grunt, halfway between amusement and disapproval. *"Understood. Well, the reason I'm calling is to confirm what the local dispatch told us—that you and your team may be in possession of... something from that research station. I don't have the exact details, but from the scuttlebutt, it's some scientific discovery. Possibly a virus?"*

Ben froze, sat phone pressed to his ear, eyes darting to the black container at his feet. *He's not sure, but he guesses.* He forced calm into his voice. "Let's just say we retrieved important samples the station was studying."

"Samples, right," Givens said, voice dropping a notch. *"Look, I'm not a scientist. I was told you might have something extremely dangerous, something the folks at that station died to protect. From what I gather, it's an old bug, maybe older than humanity. That ring any bells?"*

A wave of cold dread washed over Ben. He cast a glance at Qannik, who peered at him questioningly. No one outside the immediate circle was supposed to know details. *But apparently, word's out.* "We have an ice-core sample," Ben admitted, reluctant. "It contains a dormant virus. A lethal one, from what we've seen."

Givens exhaled, the static distorting the sound. *"Okay. That's what I thought."* He paused, as though gathering courage. *"We're staging a rescue attempt in cooperation with the Greenlandic authorities. Problem is, the storm's shifting around your coordinates. Helicopters might not get in easily. We might have to approach by ground. Are you and your people stable enough to hold out a bit longer?"*

Ben eyed the group of wounded. Ingrid was near death if they didn't get proper medical assistance. Jillian had only a partial splint. "We'll manage," he said, though doubt laced his tone. "But not for days. I've got one whose fever's out of control. She needs a hospital. Another's leg is broken. We're... we're not in great shape."

A resigned grunt came through the phone. *"Right. I'll pass that on. We'll do everything we can to expedite. We're about eight hours out, maybe less if the weather breaks. We've got a couple of Snowcat-type vehicles, plus some medical staff. They move slowly, but they've got heaters and we can turn them into makeshift ambulances."*

Ben felt a flicker of hope. "Appreciate it," he said tightly. "We also have two mercenaries tied up outside, plus one unconscious pilot. They're in bad shape too. You might wanna bring more restraints, or... I don't know."

"Noted," Givens replied. *"We can handle that. Look, I don't want to pry, but is that container of yours secure? If it's what I think it is, there might be others who'd go to great lengths to get their hands on it."*

Ben let out a short, humorless laugh. "We noticed. We've already been attacked once since the crash. The container's sealed up. I'm keeping it in sight. And in case you think rescuing us lends you credibility — it doesn't. It's not leaving my sight."

"Good," Givens said, relief in his voice. *"I won't try to argue, but I'm on the good guys' team. We'll put it under proper lock and key once we arrive, but you can ride with it. I'm no official spook, but I know the government's real anxious about that virus. Word is the White House was briefed. That's how big this got, apparently. I can show you the proper credentials and whatnot later, but you have my word — that container stays with you as long as it takes to trust me."*

Ben closed his eyes, shaking his head in frustration despite feeling a bit of relief. *So, the cat's out of the bag.* And he should have known. From the very first call he'd gotten, he'd suspected that there were others in the US government and around the world who already knew what was in the ice core samples.

And it explained the wave of interest from various mercenary outfits. If the White House had been briefed, it meant half the intelligence community might be buzzing with rumors—some might be allies, others opportunistic. "We'll hold out," he said at last. "Just get here. Ingrid's not gonna last much longer."

"I hear you," Givens replied quietly. *"I'm sorry you're in this mess, but we do appreciate it. We're doing what we can."*

Ben hesitated, a swirl of conflicting emotions threatening to choke him. He'd lost count of how many times some faceless operative or official had apologized for "the mess" while expecting them to do all the dirty work. "Fine," he managed. "We'll keep the phone on. Call if you have any updates."

"Will do. Bennett, hang in there." The line clicked off.

Ben lowered the phone, mouth set in a hard line. Qannik stood a few feet away, rifle cradled, the faint glow of the fire flickering on his features. "We have inbound," Ben said tiredly. "Some guy named Givens. Says they'll come by ground if the weather's too rough for choppers."

Qannik nodded. "How long?"

Ben shrugged. "Up to eight hours, maybe more. They said they know about the virus. Or they suspect strongly. Figures, right?"

Qannik blew out a breath, glancing at the black container. "Great. Another interested party. But if they're bringing real medics, Ingrid might pull through."

They returned to the plane, the outside wind biting at their backs. Inside, Dr. Davis had laid Ingrid on a nest of blankets, checking her temperature with a battered thermometer. Jillian stirred at the sound of their footsteps, blinking dazedly. "Any news?" she mumbled.

Ben knelt beside her. "A rescue team's coming. Ground convoy. Might take eight hours, but... they're on their way." He tried to keep the weariness out of his voice.

Her eyes fluttered with relief, though pain still etched her face. "Thank God," she whispered. "You think they'll actually make it?"

He squeezed her hand gently. "We'll find out. They claim they have medical staff. That's good enough for me."

Dr. Davis looked up from Ingrid. "Her fever's not budging. Another eight hours... it's going to be close. I'll do what I can." He dipped a rag in melted snow water, draping it over Ingrid's forehead. She stirred, lips parting in a faint gasp. Even that small movement made Ben's heart clench. She had to live.

They'd come too far for her story to end out here.

CHAPTER 24

QANNIK BUSIED himself reinforcing the plane's interior. The tail section provided some barrier against the wind, but the structure was riddled with bullet holes and cracks. He shoved more cushions and scraps of wreckage into new gaps that had formed from the windy battering. Dr. Davis rummaged for anything to help keep Ingrid's body temperature stable. Meanwhile, Jillian closed her eyes, focusing on shallow, controlled breaths to endure the pain in her leg.

At intervals, Ben stepped outside to check the fire. The mercenaries were still glowering, occasionally begging for water or a bit of heat. Qannik or Ben would toss them a piece of foam they could burn on a small side-flame, enough to keep them from freezing outright, but not enough to cut their ties or allow them a chance for mischief.

Once or twice, the mercenaries' leader—Black-Beard—tried to negotiate for release, but Ben just shook his head. If these men wanted to survive, they'd wait for the rescue team like everyone else.

The hours crawled by in a slow death march. Ben found himself nodding off near the tail, only to snap awake at the slightest sound. He checked the sat phone for calls. *Nothing.* The battery indicator still showed half full. Another slender mercy in this wasteland.

Eventually, the weak Arctic dawn spread across the sky, revealing the devastation clearly. The plane glinted in the pale light, half-buried in snow. The wind had calmed further, leaving the crash site eerily silent. Qannik's fire had dwindled to embers, so he rose to gather more debris for fuel. Ben helped, his breath puffing in the faint sun. They sparked the fire again, hoping to attract any overhead scouting aircraft—if indeed Givens's team had air support.

A sudden ring on the sat phone shattered the hush. Ben scrambled to answer. "Hello?"

Givens's voice crackled. *"We're en route. Moving faster than expected, and some local snowmobiles joined us. We might be there in an hour instead of three or four more. How's the patient?"*

Ben's heart lifted. "Thank you. Ingrid's alive, but just barely. Another hour is still pushing it. Jillian's leg might be infected if we don't set it soon."

A sympathetic pause. *"We'll keep moving."*

The line disconnected. Ben pocketed the phone, exhaling. He told Qannik and Dr. Davis about the updated ETA. Jillian blinked, managing a slight nod, as if it were an eternity but better than nothing. Ingrid lay motionless except for the faint rise and fall of her chest, cooled rags on her forehead.

Mara remained unconscious in the cockpit, unmoving. Ben had seen Dr. Davis sneak up there earlier; perhaps the man had introduced some sort of agent into her bloodstream that would keep the woman in that state.

Ben cradled the virus container on his lap, part of him hating the weight of it. This vile relic had sparked so much death. Now some new operative or official would whisk it away for safekeeping—or, cynically, for study.

And he'd been the one tasked with getting safely into their hands.

He thought of Dr. Falk's diaries, the frantic notes Ingrid and her colleagues had made about the pathogen's potential.

The memory set his teeth on edge. *We can't let them weaponize it.*

But that was a worry for tomorrow. Survival came first.

The light strengthened as the minutes crawled. With the sun came a slight rise in temperature, maybe a degree or two—enough to stave off the worst of the frostbite. Ben felt a glimmer of hope. The rescue team, if they truly had snowmobiles or snowcats, might navigate the terrain more easily now that the wind had died.

In between tasks, he stole a moment to rest his back against a chunk of plane debris, eyes half-closing. Memories flickered behind his lids: Ingrid's haunted expression when she'd first described the virus's horrifying potential, Dr. Falk's lifeless body in the station lab, the standoff with the mercenaries in the sub-level. The plane's violent crash, Jillian's screams as her leg snapped under the impact. And most recently, the firefight outside, muzzle flashes strobing in the twilight.

All for a handful of test tubes, he thought bitterly. *All for a bug no one asked to discover.*

He was jolted out of his reverie by Qannik calling his name. Blinking, he rose unsteadily. Qannik stood near the remains of the cockpit, scanning the distant snowfields. "I see something," Qannik said.

Ben joined him, squinting at the horizon. At first, he saw only the haze of ice and rock. Then, faintly, a column of white powder kicked up by approaching vehicles. It had to be the rescue party. He couldn't make out any details yet, but the movement was steady, heading right for them.

Dr. Davis leaned out of the plane's side. "That them?"

Ben felt a surge of excitement tempered by caution. "Probably. Let's be ready in case it isn't."

They armed themselves, though half the rifles they'd collected from the mercenary group were low on ammo. There were likely a few more magazines on the bodies of the fallen men outside, but they didn't have time to check. The two mercenaries they'd tied up, sensing something, stirred and muttered among themselves. Qannik brandished his weapon at them, ensuring no one tried to break free.

The shapes in the distance coalesced into actual vehicles—two large track-based transports and a pair of snowmobiles.

Finally, the lead vehicle churned to a stop about fifty yards away. Men in heavy jackets and goggles hopped out, scanning the wreckage.

No weapons.

That was good to see. *Maybe they* are *here to rescue us,* Ben thought.

One of the men raised an arm in greeting. Ben noticed the figure wore a medical armband. A second figure stepped forward, smaller, wearing a thick parka with the hood pulled low. "Bennett?" a voice shouted.

Ben stepped away from cover, container in hand. "Yeah!"

The second figure advanced, flipping down his hood. A middle-aged man, bearded, with a lean face that hinted at both exhaustion and relief. "I'm Givens," he called, chest rising with quick breaths. "We spoke on the phone. We've got medical supplies and a team to get you out."

Ben released a breath he hadn't realized he was holding. Behind Givens, half a dozen others were unloading stretchers, medical kits, and a swirl of gear. "We have two critical," Ben said. "One with a broken leg, one near organ failure from a severe fever. Potentially infected with whatever... *this* is." He nodded his head toward the container of virus samples. "Another one's unconscious up front in the cockpit. And a handful of hostiles." He waved at the mercenaries, who stared back sullenly.

Givens nodded sharply, motioning for a medic to follow. "We'll take care of them. Show us to your wounded first."

In quick, efficient movements, they turned the plane site into a triage zone. One medic rushed to Ingrid, exclaiming under his breath at her high temperature. They loaded her onto a fresh gurney, hooking up an IV with more broad-spectrum antibiotics and giving her a portable oxygen supply. Jillian hissed through clenched teeth as they shifted her onto a second stretcher, her leg carefully cradled. She was pale, but her eyes flickered with relief.

CHAPTER 25

GIVENS HOVERED NEAR BEN, occasionally checking that everything was secure. "Where's that pilot?" he asked.

Ben pointed to the cockpit. "She betrayed us. She's not to be trusted. She's the reason we're all here, and our plane went down."

Givens nodded. The rescue team found Mara slumped there, coaxing her onto a stretcher as well. Meanwhile, two men appeared who were armed — pistols, but they kept them holstered. They took charge of the bound mercenaries, reading them some basic rights in a clipped, half-official tone. The mercenaries spat and glared, but they didn't resist.

Finally, Givens looked at the black container. His gaze lingered, but he didn't reach for it. "That's it, isn't it? The thing the station died for."

Ben pressed his lips together. "It's dangerous. We keep it locked until we're sure it's safe."

Givens nodded, swallowing. "I get it. The authorities want it quarantined ASAP."

Ben bristled at the word "authorities." He'd seen too much chaos. But right now, the priority was Ingrid's survival, Jillian's well-being, and ensuring no more mercenaries tried to snatch the virus. *A bigger fight can happen later,* he told himself. "It was *quarantined* just fine a mile beneath the ice. Too bad I can't just drop it back down the hole it came out of."

"Too bad."

Ben grunted. "We can talk details once we're out of here."

"Agreed," Givens said softly. Then he lifted his radio, barking orders to his team to load Ingrid and Jillian into the tracked vehicle. Dr. Davis climbed in with them, not letting Ingrid out of his sight. Qannik helped oversee the captive mercenaries and Mara.

One of the rescue team rummaged for sedation drugs in case the mercs got rowdy in their snowcat.

Before Ben followed them into the vehicle, he paused, letting a swirl of wind ruffle his hair. The sun was stronger now, glinting off jagged ice ridges. He took a moment to look at the broken plane—its crushed metal shimmering in the daylight, the bullet holes pocked along the side, the twisted cockpit where this entire last stand had played out. A sense of finality washed over him, though he knew that once they were out of Greenland, the real negotiations over the virus might begin. Still, they had survived, and that counted for something.

He turned away, stepping carefully through the snow, the container tight against his side. Givens stood by the open bay of the lead tracked vehicle, waving him in. The inside looked cramped but warm, with benches lining the walls. He'd been in vehicles like it before — one that he'd not-so-ceremoniously ridden off an avalanche and over a cliff in Norway.

Let's not repeat that today, he thought.

Jillian and Ingrid were already strapped into portable cots, the medics hooking up IV lines and monitors. Mara lay in the corner, eyes still shut, a paramedic shining a flashlight into her pupils. Dr. Davis hovered between Ingrid and Jillian, face etched with worry and relief in equal measure.

Qannik helped load the last of their gear—what little they had—then joined them. The two armed men forced the captured mercenaries into a second vehicle. Givens hopped in last, slamming the heavy door against the biting wind. With a rumble, the machine lurched into motion, treads grinding over snow and ice.

Inside, the heat felt almost suffocating after so long in the cold. Ben sank onto a bench, letting the container rest between his feet. He couldn't bring himself to relax fully, but he felt some tension slip away. Jillian offered a weak nod, one hand raised in a semblance of a thumbs-up. Ingrid's chest rose and fell under an oxygen mask, color faintly returning to her cheeks. Dr. Davis, leaning over them, gave Ben a small, grateful nod.

Givens took a seat across from Ben, breathing heavily. "We'll get to a field hospital about two hours from here," he explained. "Then we can arrange a flight to a real base. After that... well, that's above my pay grade, but from what I hear, the US wants you stateside. No one's telling me exactly why, but I can guess." He flicked a glance at the container.

Ben folded his arms, ignoring the dull ache in his ribs. "We appreciate the rescue," he said simply.

Givens's lips curved in a tight half-smile. "Glad to do it. Let's just hope we can keep your friend alive." He nodded toward Ingrid. "She looks in rough shape."

The hum of the engine filled the space, drowning conversation. Ben leaned back, exhaustion weighing down his eyelids. He glanced at Qannik, who sat near the door, rifle across his knees. His friend gave a small, resigned shrug—*We made it, for now.* Jillian and Ingrid were in medical hands, the mercenaries under guard. Mara, ironically, was receiving the same medical care she would have denied them. And the virus container was safe, for better or worse.

Outside, the treads of the vehicle crunched across the tundra, jostling them all with each bump. The day's thin sunlight glowed through the reinforced windows. Ben felt the tension in his muscles begin to ebb. They were leaving the crash site, leaving behind a trail of bullet casings and broken metal, and hauling away a cargo that might change the fate of humanity if it ever got loose. But at least no one else would die out here under these brutal skies, or so he hoped.

He settled back, letting his eyes drift shut for a moment, lulled by the steady rumble. The battered container nudged his foot, as though reminding him it was still there. He didn't need the reminder; he knew all too well what they'd gone through to protect it.

Maybe soon, he thought, *someone else can carry this burden.* Because for now, he'd done enough. If Givens and his men wanted to handle the aftermath, and they were who he said they were — let them. He just wanted to get back to Julie and Hope.

And a hot shower that lasted a year.

As the snowcat lumbered on through the frozen expanse, the tension in the cabin softened, replaced by a weary sense of relief. Qannik exhaled and shut his eyes, letting the rifle rest across his lap. Dr. Davis continued monitoring the wounded. Givens quietly spoke into a handheld radio, updating some unseen dispatch about their progress.

Ben allowed himself one final look at Ingrid's face, noting the faint color already coming back to her cheeks. Then he closed his eyes, ignoring every ache and bruise. The cold gloom of Greenland still surrounded them, but for the first time since they'd left the station, it felt like they were truly leaving death behind and pressing on toward life.

And that was enough—at least for now.

CHAPTER 26

BEN STOOD by a wall of windows in a private hospital room, staring past the glass at the subdued bustle of a small airfield. The building was more functional than luxurious—clearly designed for remote deployments and triage rather than long-term care—but right now, it felt like a palace compared to the freezing chaos from which they'd come.

A few days had passed since the rescue, yet to Ben, it all still felt unreal.

A dull ache settled into his ribs every time he moved, souvenirs from the plane crash and the brawls before it. Splotches of bruising marked his arms like strange tattoos, faded from purple to sickly green. As he shifted position, he caught his reflection in the window: hollow eyes, hair cropped shorter than usual — he'd let a medic trim away the blood-matted snarls — and a scar on his temple.

He barely recognized himself.

He'd called Julie and told her everything, and that he'd be home as soon as possible. Givens checked out; at least to Ben, he did seem to be an employee of the Department of Defense with a high enough security clearance that his answers to Ben's questions had become shorter, and eventually useless. But he'd kept his end of the bargain, and that was more than enough for Ben. He'd informed Ben that he was shipping out later; another man named Carlos Chambers — the man he'd first spoken with on the phone back in Anchorage — would be stepping in to finalize transport of the container and tie up loose ends.

Ben didn't care, it was a typical government play: more bureaucracy than any mere mortal could keep track of, seemingly for just the sake of bureaucracy. He figured it was as simple as the more players who touched the football, the more players got credit.

He turned from the glass to look at Ingrid, lying in the bed behind him. Her face was gaunt, but her color had improved drastically. A tangle of IV lines and monitors looped around her arms, feeding antibiotics and fluids. She'd made it through surgery and post-crash infections, and though she was still pale, she looked more like a living person than a ghost.

Dr. Davis had watched over her like a hawk, barely sleeping these past few nights.

He'd confirmed that it was a viral agent working itself to death in her system, and he also confirmed Ingrid's suspicions from when they'd found her: any more than what she'd accidentally been exposed to would have killed her, and likely would have jumped hosts from her to one of them.

Through the half-open door, Ben heard a quiet bustle in the hallway: doctors and nurses speaking a mixture of Danish, English, and Greenlandic; patients being wheeled in and out of rooms. This facility—somewhere on the outskirts of Kangerlussuaq—was more of a provisional hospital than a major medical center, but it had everything they needed. After the rescue, they'd flown here in a larger cargo plane once Ingrid and Jillian were stable enough to move. Now, the staff hustled to handle the fallout.

Ben took a slow breath. That black container—the reason so many people had died—had been moved to secure storage. He'd personally overseen its handoff to the facility's top-level containment unit, under guard by local authorities and some plainclothes men who'd introduced themselves in clipped American accents. The container was still sealed, and no one had yet cracked it open. Apparently, they were awaiting specialized transport to whisk it away to some stateside lab with deeper pockets and thicker walls.

And apparently, though this place wasn't American, Givens was the de facto leader — no one questioned his orders.

He shook his head, turning back to Ingrid as she stirred. Her eyes fluttered open. For a moment, she blinked at him, disoriented, then a ghost of recognition flitted across her features.

"Ben?" she whispered, voice raspy.

He stepped to her bedside. "Hey," he murmured. "You're awake. How you feeling?"

She let out a shaky breath, words sluggish. "Like someone... stuffed cotton in my head. Everything hurts."

"Sounds about right," Ben said, fighting the urge to smile. It was enough that she was coherent at all. "You're in a hospital. Dr. Davis has been here the whole time, making sure you're stable. The infection's receding."

She closed her eyes, relief evident. "The virus?"

"Safe. Locked down. You did it," he said. "We all did."

A faint exhale, like a laugh that never fully formed. "Good. That means no one else can... weaponize it."

He didn't answer that part. They both knew that was the fear: that this ancient pathogen *could* be turned into a biological nightmare. People had died trying to prevent that possibility. And knowing what he did about governments, he suspected that's exactly what his would do.

Hopefully, they'd just study the thing, try to figure it out and perhaps how, *theoretically*, they might turn it into a weapon.

Theoretically.

At least for now, the virus was still sealed in its vials. Whether that was cause for celebration or dread, Ben couldn't say.

The door eased open, and Dr. Davis slipped in, wearing rumpled scrubs. He carried a small tray of fresh bandages and medicine. "She's awake?" he asked softly.

Ben nodded, stepping aside so Davis could check Ingrid's vitals. She managed a weak smile for him, and the doctor returned it with genuine warmth. "We've been waiting for you to snap out of that fever," he murmured, kneeling to re-tape an IV line near her wrist. "You gave us a scare."

She licked chapped lips. "You saved me, Chuck. Thank you."

Ben saw something in Dr. Davis' gaze he'd missed before. *They aren't just colleagues*, he realized. He wasn't sure *what* exactly they were, but they looked at each other now the way people who are more than friends look at one another.

Davis shrugged off the compliment. "Just doing my job. Plus, you did plenty of the saving yourself, from what I hear about the station. Don't try to speak too much yet, you need rest."

Ingrid closed her eyes, letting out a sigh that sounded more peaceful than in the past days. Davis tucked a blanket around her shoulders, then turned to Ben with a quiet nod—"She's improving," that nod seemed to say, "but let her rest." Ben got the message and followed Davis back into the hallway.

Outside, the corridor was all white tile and fluorescent lighting, bustling with staff. Ben wondered if this was the busiest this place had ever been. They found a corner near a vending machine. Davis keyed in for a cup of coffee, running a hand through his thinning hair. "I can't believe how close we came to losing her," he admitted. "If those snow cats, or that helicopter after, had been an hour later..."

Ben swallowed that particular nightmare. "But it *wasn't*," he said, voice tight. "We made it."

Davis nodded, letting out a breath. "And Jillian?"

"Recovering in the next ward," Ben said. "She hates the bed rest, but the docs say she'll need at least two months of rehab. The leg was a clean break, but the crash made it tricky. She had some internal bleeding too."

The coffee machine spat a cup of steaming liquid. Davis took it, sipping carefully. "Better than I expected. Good old Jillian. As stubborn as they come."

Ben allowed a tiny smile, remembering Jillian's sarcasm even in the darkest hours. "She'll be back on her feet eventually. A crutch, maybe. Nothing permanent."

Davis exhaled. "Thank God."

CHAPTER 27

THEY TURNED as a commotion echoed from down the hall: the squeak of a wheelchair and a familiar voice. Qannik rolled around the corner, pushing Mara in a chair, an orderly trailing behind with a disapproving scowl. Mara's head was wrapped in a bandage, eyes half-lidded from pain meds. Qannik, sporting a sling for his shoulder, gave them a dry, exasperated look.

"She insisted on getting out of bed," Qannik said, jabbing a thumb at Mara. "Nurses said no, she said yes. This was the compromise."

Ben steeled himself, then arched an eyebrow. He wasn't quite sure what to make of their turncoat pilot. "Mara, you can't even walk yet."

Mara glowered, though exhaustion undercut her usual sharpness. "I can't lie in bed forever," she rasped. "I need to talk to you. About... everything." Her gaze flitted nervously between them. The fear or guilt in her expression was new; she usually wore the face of someone in control.

Ben folded his arms. "We'll talk. But you almost killed us — *all* of us. Not exactly something that's easily forgiven."

She winced, turning her head away. Qannik patted her shoulder with mock sympathy. "Karma, yes?"

"Yeah," she muttered. "I get it. But I'm not trying to apologize. I know that's useless. But maybe explain. Can we find someplace quiet?"

The orderly behind them cleared his throat. "She's not cleared to wander, sir. Ten minutes, that's it."

Mara waved him off, though her arm trembled. "Enough. Let me talk."

Davis exchanged a glance with Ben, then beckoned them toward a small waiting lounge at the end of the corridor. Qannik rolled Mara's wheelchair inside, parking it near a table stacked with medical pamphlets. Ben crossed the threshold, arms still folded. She wanted to talk; he'd let her. But he wasn't sure what she could possibly say to excuse what she'd done.

Mara grimaced as she tried to straighten in the wheelchair. "Look," she said, voice subdued, "I know I can't fix what happened. I made a deal... thought I'd get enough money to skip out of this cold-ass place forever. I was tired of being a contract pilot, you know? Sounds exotic at first, but... Anyway, I never wanted you dead. Honest."

Ben nearly laughed, incredulous. "You held us at gunpoint. You threatened Ingrid's life if we didn't hand over the container."

She gave a weak shrug, tears sparking in her eyes. "I *panicked*. That virus is worth... You have *no idea*. And I'm stuck in Greenland, beholden to some bad people, with debts I can't pay. It seemed like the only way out."

Qannik let out a quiet snort. "Good plan, right?"

Mara ignored him, looking at Ben. "Then it all went to hell. The storm, the crash... Look, I'm not asking forgiveness. I know what I did, and I know it's not forgivable. But I'm *done* with that life. Nurse says I might lose partial hearing in my left ear from the crash, and my flying days are probably over. I'll have to sell my plane to settle up with..." Her lips pressed into a tight line, and Ben saw a tear forming in her eye. "Whatever. Serves me right."

Ben studied her. The old anger still boiled in him, but there was a twinge of pity, too. She'd let greed overshadow everything else, sure, but now she was in a hospital bed with multiple fractures and a head injury. "What do you want from me?"

Her gaze flickered to the hallway. "I figure you'll have me arrested. You've probably already told everyone that I'm damaged goods, or even with that merc group you took out. Figure it's just a matter of time before the cops bust in and roll me away. I just... wanted to say if you need to track down who I was dealing with, I'll give you names. I'm done protecting them. Might help you keep that virus locked up."

Ben exchanged a look with Qannik. Then Davis. Qannik shrugged as if to say, *Up to you*. Davis simply stared, not interfering. Ben sighed, bracing a hand on the back of a plastic chair. "The virus is safe. Locked up, and —"

"You know how this stuff works, Bennett," she said. "Yeah, fine, *this* virus is safe. But are *you*?" She turned to Davis. "You think you can just go back to the way it was? Now that we all know there was *something* down there, in that ice, they're going to be scrambling to get it."

"Who?"

"The buyers I had lined up, other interested parties, governments. *Everyone*. I'm just asking you to get my contact's info. Maybe you can do something about them, maybe not. I'm hoping it just goes a little ways toward making things right."

"All right, Mara. We'll talk later, once Ingrid and Jillian are stable. Maybe your info can keep a few mercs off your back, and ours. Meanwhile, rest. The doctors say you're not going anywhere soon."

She swallowed hard, glancing at the bandages across her ribs. "Right." Then, eyes wet, she rasped, "For whatever it's worth... I *am* sorry."

Ben stood silent for a moment. Then he gestured at Qannik. "Take her back. She needs real rest."

Qannik nodded, rolling Mara's chair around as the orderly stepped in. She gave Ben one last look—a mess of regret, fear, and some lingering spark of defiance. Then they disappeared into the corridor. Dr. Davis exhaled, turning to Ben. "Think we can trust her to not pull another stunt?"

Ben shrugged. "She can't even walk without help. I don't think she'll be hijacking any planes soon." He paused. "But I'll warn the staff to keep an eye on her anyway."

CHAPTER 28

THEY DRIFTED BACK to Ingrid's room, passing doctors and uniformed security along the way. The hall had a half-dozen American men in plain suits stationed near the facility's exits—probably the same group who took the container into a locked storeroom. Ben guessed they were mid-level government or private contractors, all hush-hush. He recognized one from the day they'd arrived, a man with a short mustache who nodded politely each time Ben passed.

Inside Ingrid's room, the hush felt more comforting than oppressive. She was dozing again, chest rising and falling with minimal strain. A nurse quietly checked her IV drip. Dr. Davis drifted to the window, gazing at the same runway Ben had studied earlier. Ben sank into a stiff chair, letting the tension in his shoulders uncoil.

"You look like you could use some real rest, too," Davis murmured, not taking his eyes off the view.

Ben rubbed his face, then laughed. "You know I've got a one-year-old at home? Yeah, I could use some *real* rest. Whatever that is."

Davis laughed.

"Soon. I just..." Ben paused, swallowing thickly. "I still feel like *something's* unresolved. That container. The last wave of mercenaries. The station."

Davis's nod was slow. "I know. But you did what you set out to do: keep that virus from being exploited. Ingrid's alive because *you* insisted on a rescue. Jillian's going to walk again. Let yourself rest, as much as you can."

Ben tried to let those words sink in. He closed his eyes, remembering the swirl of chaos—the station's sub-level, the crash, the firefight, the final helicopter. *We survived.* That had to count for something. Ingrid had a second chance, Jillian would eventually limp out of here, and even Qannik had come out with only a minor shoulder injury. Mara was grounded, but breathing. The container was locked away. Possibly it would disappear into some clandestine lab; possibly a new set of problems would arise. But for now, his crisis was over.

He drifted into a half-doze. After a while, the nurse gently tapped his shoulder, urging him to move to a couch in the next room if he wanted to sleep. Dr. Davis remained by Ingrid's side, speaking softly to her when she stirred. Ben stumbled out, found the couch, and collapsed into a dreamless slumber.

He awoke hours later to see a watery sun high in the sky through the nearest window. The temperature had risen slightly, leaving the edges of the tarmac glistening with meltwater. As he shook off the grogginess, footsteps approached, and a figure in a neat black coat appeared. A man in his forties, with close-cropped black hair and a calm bearing—a cut above the typical local staff.

Ben immediately recognized that intangible hush-hush vibe.

Possibly American.

Possibly from the same network of "friends" who'd roped him into the station fiasco in the first place.

"Bennett?" the man asked quietly.

Ben rose, wincing at the stiffness in his back. "Yeah, that's me. You are...?"

The man offered a small smile that didn't reach his eyes. "Carlos Chambers. We spoke on the phone before all of this. I work with Givens. May we speak in private?"

Ben narrowed his eyes. "He mentioned you. Not sure we have anything to discuss that can't be said right here."

Chambers gave a gracious nod, stepping aside so two passing nurses could wheel a patient past. "Very well," he said, lowering his voice. "I'll be brief. My superiors want to express gratitude for your efforts. The virus is contained, thanks to you. We're arranging transport to a higher-security facility stateside. Givens informed me you were a bit stubborn when it comes to moving this thing around, so I'd just like to confirm your role in the handoff."

Ben chewed the inside of his cheek. "I'll be there for whatever handoff you've got planned, sure. But I'm no scientist. Ingrid's the one who discovered it, and she almost died protecting it. If you want anyone's blessing, it's hers."

Chambers inclined his head. "We're not asking for blessings—just ensuring there's no confusion about chain of custody. Givens respects you, so I have no reason not to as well. But this *is* now the property of the United States Department of Defense. We'll file the necessary paperwork with the local authorities, and I wanted to make sure you were there to see it. As for Dr. Ingrid... we'd be happy for her input when she's stable enough. A specialized team is flying in soon."

Something about the man's clinical tone made Ben's skin crawl. He forced himself to remain polite. "All right. Long as it stays sealed. I don't want that thing used or tested on humans."

Chambers gave a noncommittal shrug. "I'm not at liberty to discuss specifics.

But you can rest assured we *are* taking every precaution. This find really is a matter of national security. Possibly global security. It needs to stay with the good guys."

Ben let out a heavy breath. "Yeah, I know." He paused, then asked quietly, "What about the people who died? Dr. Falk and the rest. They deserve some acknowledgment."

A flicker of something passed over Chambers' face. Guilt, maybe. "Their families will be informed of the official story: a tragic research accident, remote location, harsh conditions. The usual disclaimers. We can't exactly publicize the existence of a pandemic-grade virus. It would cause a global panic."

Ben tensed. "They deserve more than a footnote."

Chambers exhaled, voice gentler now. "I understand. Sometimes the best we can do is honor them in ways the public won't ever see. But their sacrifice won't be forgotten, at least not by the people who matter." He glanced at Ben's battered figure, as if evaluating him anew. "As for you, the CSO, Dr. Chuck Davis, Dr. Jillian Shepherd, and the rest... we'll see to your needs. Let's just say we have ways of expressing gratitude."

"Right," Ben muttered. "Well, put it in writing. My organization is always looking for funding and — I'm sure you understand — *contacts*. And as soon as Ingrid's stable, she gets a say in what you guys cook up with that virus. If you need my help, I'll be around. Otherwise, I'm done with it."

Chambers nodded, as if that was a fair statement. "Understood. Here," he said, sliding a small card from his pocket. "My number. If you need anything, or if someone else tries to take the container."

Ben took the card, blinking at the plain text: a phone number, no name. *Typical*. "Thanks. We done?"

A faint smile ghosted across Chambers' lips. "For now. I'll let you rest." He offered a stiff half-bow, then turned and melted into the hallway throng, leaving Ben to wonder if the entire conversation had been a dream. He glanced at the card, shaking his head in weary disbelief.

CHAPTER 29

LATER THAT AFTERNOON, Ben sat by Jillian's bed in another wing of the building. She looked irritated but better rested than the day before, a cast on her leg and an IV drip in her arm. "They say I can't walk for eight weeks," she complained. "You know how many flight connections I'll miss?"

Ben snorted softly, adjusting the pillow behind her back. "Guess you'll have to stay put. You've earned some downtime. But hey, look on the bright side. I overhead two nurses talking, and they mentioned they've got tablets with *Netflix* on them. They *did* say the internet was near-useless, though. But hey. Netflix!"

She rolled her eyes and groaned, though there was a gratitude in her smile. "I remember the crash, bits of it. Then not much after. I can't believe we're out of that frozen tomb."

"Me neither," Ben admitted.

She yawned, letting her head loll back. "Once I'm better, maybe I'll ask Ingrid if she wants to finish what they started—studying the virus in a safe lab. She's the only one who truly understands the scope."

Ben frowned. "That's up to her. Though I doubt she'll want to dive back into research that nearly killed her."

Jillian's gaze turned thoughtful. "Well, I'm not so sure. For a scientist like her... sometimes knowledge is worth it. We'll see."

He offered a gentle shrug. "First, you heal."

She nodded, eyes half-closed again as the medication lulled her to drowsiness. "Thanks, Ben," she murmured. "For not letting me die out there."

He squeezed her hand, not trusting himself to speak without emotion churning up. He'd never been much of an emotional guy, but after having Hope, he'd softened quite a bit.

He quietly slipped out, letting her rest.

That evening, Qannik found Ben in the hospital's canteen, picking at a tray of bland but warm food. Qannik's arm remained in a sling, but his posture was otherwise strong. He took a seat across from Ben, motioning to the half-empty plate. "No appetite?"

Ben forced a wry smile. "I keep thinking about all the times we almost starved or froze. Now we have hot meals. But it's like my stomach still hasn't settled, and it's expecting frozen tree bark or a pinecone, instead of real food."

Qannik hummed in agreement, glancing around at the small cluster of staff. "You hear what they're doing with the container?"

Ben stabbed a piece of boiled potato. "Yeah. Some hush-hush transport state-side. The same spooks who paid for that chopper and snowcat rescue, I assume. That Chambers guy said they'll 'keep it safe.'" He made air quotes with his free hand.

Qannik's lips curved in a faint grin. "You trust them? Givens?"

Ben shrugged. "I think I do trust Givens. I'm coming around on Chambers, especially since he hasn't contradicted anything Givens has said so far. But better them than the mercenaries. We might not get a perfect outcome, but at least it's not on the black market. Ingrid's alive to keep them honest, if she chooses to weigh in on the scientific side."

They fell into companionable silence, the relief of survival clashing with the knowledge that the world had nearly glimpsed a cataclysmic threat. After a while, Qannik spoke again. "What about you? Just going right back to the CSO?"

Ben thought of the phone calls, the frantic rescue, the unending sense of being a pawn in a bigger game. "I don't know," he admitted. "This fiasco taught me a lot, mostly that I hate being in the dark. But I've always thought that if I can keep good people alive, it's worth it. And hell, this *is* the CSO — every damn time, we end up over our heads." He laughed. "Just once I'd like a mission that's akin to walking into a grocery store and picking a ripe apple to buy. Easy, simple. No trouble."

Qannik nodded slowly, eyes distant as if recalling the ice storms and firefights. "I fear your role on this planet might be more important than picking good apples."

"I fear you're right, buddy," Ben said. "What about you?"

"I might go back to guiding, but not for a while. Need to let the shoulder heal." A small, ironic laugh escaped him. "Had enough 'adventure' to last a life-time. But..."

Ben waited.

"This CSO thing, it seems like a pretty good gig."

"You mean, *besides* getting shot at by mercenaries? And plane crashes?"

"First time for everything," Qannik said.

"Believe it or not, that wasn't my first time for either. But yeah, it's a pretty good gig. Why?"

"You ever think you'd need someone like me?"

Ben paused, sizing the man up. "Absolutely. You interested?"

"I'll give you my number. I'd love to help with... whatever it is you get caught up in. But maybe after we heal up."

They both smirked. Then Ben reached out and clapped Qannik's uninjured shoulder. "We're alive. Let's take that as a victory."

CHAPTER 30

THE NEXT MORNING, Ingrid insisted on sitting up in bed. Dr. Davis, looking amused, helped prop her with pillows. Her hair was washed, eyes brighter despite lingering fatigue. Ben sat at her bedside while Davis did a final check of her IV line.

She mustered a smile, though it wavered with emotion. "I heard the container's gone. The virus, the ice sample... all of it."

Ben nodded. "They flew it out. Carlos Chambers and his crew. Probably locked in a high-security lab by now."

A flicker of sadness crossed her face, but also relief. "Good. I'd hoped to study it more, but after everything... maybe it's best."

Ben folded his arms. "If you want to follow up, I'm sure they'd value your input. Chambers might let you consult. But that's your call."

She closed her eyes, remembering the horrors beneath the station. "I think I need time before I stare into another microscope. People died because we poked too deep. Maybe I should study something safer—like ice cores from Mars, or some fruit flies." A faint, weary chuckle.

Ben gently rested a hand on her blanket-covered knee. "Whatever you choose, at least you have the chance. I'm glad you're alive."

Her eyes shone with gratitude. "Me too. Thank you, Ben." She paused, swallowing. "For everything."

They fell into a companionable silence, the tension of days past easing into acceptance. Eventually, Dr. Davis ushered Ben out so Ingrid could rest. He left with a lighter heart, confident Ingrid would walk out of this hospital eventually, free to decide her future. The virus, for now, wasn't her burden alone.

In the following hours, final arrangements were made. Jillian was cleared for a flight stateside. Ingrid would stay a bit longer before she could travel, too. Qannik decided to remain in Greenland and recover near his extended family in a smaller coastal town, all expenses paid thanks to a mysterious source that simply had the address of the nearest US Embassy listed on the check. Dr. Chuck Davis planned to accompany Jillian, ensuring her leg healed properly.

Ben booked a ticket that left a day after Jillian's flight.

Half a world away, as soon as Ben landed in Anchorage, he was met outside the terminal by both Givens and Chambers.

"Bennett," Chambers greeted, that neutral tone returning.

Ben stuffed his hands in his coat pockets. "Leaving soon?"

Chambers nodded. "Yes. I was confirming the last detail: the container is still en route to a Department of Defense facility in the U.S. The path is hush-hush, multiple stops to avoid prying eyes."

Ben inhaled the cold air. "Good luck keeping it quiet."

Chambers offered a wan smile. "We'll do our best. I just wanted to say—on behalf of those who orchestrated the rescue—thank you. We know you didn't sign up for half of what transpired."

Ben laughed without humor. "Yeah, well. Here we are."

Chambers hesitated, then reached into an inside coat pocket, withdrawing a sealed envelope. "This is for you. A small compensation, though more formal arrangements will follow once we've written everything up."

Ben eyed the envelope, uncertain. "Money?"

Givens shrugged, stepping in. "A start. Also a letter from our employer, expressing official gratitude. And a private contact number if you need anything else. We take care of our own, and I'd consider you one of our own. I know you've done work for the US government before, but current DoD brass is a little more encouraging of this sort of off-the-books work. I'd like to keep you in our stable, just in case."

Ben took the envelope, turning it over in his fingers. A swirl of conflicting emotions rose: relief that they might be compensated for near-death experiences, anger that it came as hush money, gratitude that Ingrid's hospital bills might be covered. He nodded once, not trusting himself to speak.

Chambers gave him a final, polite dip of the head. "Safe travels home, Bennett. If we need you again... you know how these things go."

Ben forced a tight smile. "Yeah," he said. "I do."

Then the two men walked away, disappearing into a waiting SUV that rumbled off the property. The wind whistled across the fence, and the last rays of sunlight bathed the snowy ground in gold. Ben stood there, envelope in hand, feeling something akin to closure, though it wasn't perfect.

In his line of work, closure was hard to come by.

He *knew* he'd be hearing from them again — likely very soon.

His cell buzzed, and he pulled it from his pocket. *Julie.*

He answered, relieved to hear his wife's voice. She gave a quick update, telling him everything Hope had gotten into that day.

"Hey, Jules — I'm on my way to my truck now. Should be home before dinner. What are you making?"

She laughed. "I thought breakfast for dinner sounded fun. How does a stack of pancakes sound?"

www.ingramcontent.com/pod-product-compliance
Lightning Source LLC
Chambersburg PA
CBHW030944310726
48969CB00008B/2380